GIVING A GANGSTA A PIECE OF MY LOVE

NIDDA

SYNOPSIS:

Milan Simmons is married to her high school sweetheart and has a career that she loves, working with youth in the juvenile system. Milan has it all until she finds out the man that she has given her all to for years has been hiding secrets from her. Milan is forced into a position where she has to choose herself and walk away from her past.

Maurice "Nightmare" Rogers is every woman's dream and every nigga's worst nightmare. Being at the top of the food chain, he is in a position that many people want, but they couldn't fill his size twelves even if he took them off of his feet and gave them to them. Runnin' the streets with an iron fist and raising a teenage daughter isn't easy, but he gets the job done.

When Milan and Nightmare cross paths, he immediately has her attention. Coming out of a bad situation, she isn't looking for what she seems to keep stumbling across with Nightmare. Once Nightmare reels her in with his thuggish abrasiveness, she just can't seem to get rid of him, even though she tries to. Milan quickly finds herself giving a gangsta a piece of her love.

Chapter One

MAURICE "NIGHTMARE" ROGERS

I made my way into Ike's simple two-story home with my brother Gunna right behind me, not even acknowledging the bitch that let us in. It took more than a fat ass and pretty face for a bitch to impress me. She should've been bowing down and kissing my shoes when I walked in this bitch because I made all the shit that she was enjoying possible. But she didn't fuck up; her nigga did, and she was goin' to suffer the consequences as well.

The bitch led the way to the back of the home. I'd never been here, switching about to knock her damn hip out of place.

"You need to save that shit for somebody that would even buy yo' ass a four for four. Bitch, I wouldn't give you change if you were beggin' for it with a sign with yo' newborn," I spat in disgust.

"Nothin' is worse than a disrespectful ass bitch," Gunna threw in as we made it to where Ike was sitting deep in thought in what appeared to be a wooden den.

"Ike!" I spat because I didn't have time for this bullshit for sure.

"Oh, wassup, Nightmare and Gunna?" Ike asked, leaning back in his pleather ass recliner.

I never thought that I would be in this position with him. I took him under my wing when this nigga was young. He started off running my corner when I wasn't able to, and I never had to question his judgement. Every move that Ike made was thought out and calculated. He wasn't in this shit to get the latest shoes and other bullshit. He was doing it to feed himself, and that was similar to me, but I had two other mouths to feed.

Somewhere along the way, this nigga lost his way and got caught up. He turned into the type of nigga to make sure that he had every Jordan that hit the store on Saturday but didn't even take pride in the place he laid his head at every night. As I made my way through his house, I peeped all types of flawed shit that the nigga I used to know wouldn't have settled for.

"Look Nigh—" Ike attempted to say as I plopped down on the couch, but once he looked up in my face, he decided to shut the fuck up.

His bitch hurried away after she noticed that things weren't going as she hoped they would. Money was the only reason that nigga was able to pull that bitch. When he was a broke ass nigga with his shoes busted and floodin', she wouldn't have looked that nigga's way. He didn't even catch any of the hints. Five babies later and a bunch of money spent, she was still tryin' to throw that pussy at any nigga that might be able to be extra income. She'd only even seen me a few times, so she had no idea she was wasting her fucking time.

"What I'm trying to figure out is why would you have some nigga that hasn't been approved by Gunna touching my shit?" I spat, because the rest of this shit didn't matter.

"It's my cousin. Man, if I would have known he was going to be on this bullshit, I wouldn't have never asked him to do it. I gave him detailed instructions to make sure he handled everything correctly. The nigga looks just like me, so he used my license to get the rental. Nightmare, man, my girl's water broke and—"

"Nigga, I don't give a fuck about yo' bitch or that gremlin big head ass baby!"

"If you had a nine to five, what would you have done if you couldn't make it to work?"

"Nigga, what the fuck are you thinking about? This is a simple fuckin' question!"

"I should have let Gunna know the situation," Ike finally spit out.

"Then why the fuck didn't you do that?" Gunna finally asked, because the tension in the room was thick, and this nigga Ike was now sweating.

"Because you didn't think I would find out." I answered

for him because a minute had passed, and he still hadn't uttered a fuckin' word.

"You got an hour to come up with my money. And then I'm goin' to make this a nightmare for yo' fam," I assured him, staring into his eyes.

Ike looked over at Gunna, hoping that he could say somethin' to change my mind. I knew my brother, and if he could do anything, it would be done. Him and Ike had been cool since kindergarten, but there was nothin' that could be said to make this shit right. The incense they were burning had my fucking head hurting worse than the fact that my shit was gone.

Ike used to be one of my top men. That was why he was supposed to be making a delivery to my nigga Lil' Murda in Kansas. He took the trip every week with no problem. Now, all of a sudden, he thought his cousin could do his job. I stood up to make my way out this nigga Ike's house.

As I made my way back out through the same route I came in this bitch, I could hear his bitch crying. She could save them tears for when they would really matter. I walked past the kitchen, and Ike's teenage daughter, that was the same age as mine, mugged the fuck out of me.

"Boo!" I spat, making her jump and fall out of the chair she was sitting in, which surprised me because she was a big one.

"Don't talk to my daddy like that!" Ike's bad ass son yelled, standing in front of the door, stopping me from leaving once I made it to the front door.

"Shut the fuck up! Take yo' ass upstairs!" Ike yelled from behind me.

"You better get yo' ET looking ass out my face and the fuck out my way," I spat, and when his skinny, funny looking ass didn't move fast enough, I moved his ass and made my way out.

"Where the fuck did that skinny nigga come from? All of Ike's kids are big," Gunna said as we cut through the grass to get to his truck.

"Stop talking to me. You know where that lil' nigga came from just like we all do. Another nigga's sack!" I yelled as I opened the passenger side door and saw Ike lookin' like a lost puppy.

"Man, don't you think that it's another way that we can handle this shit? We've known this nigga for damn near all of our lives. He fucked up once, and just like that, you just gon' get rid of him. That nigga got kids. What if somebody put Amayah in the situation you are going to put his seeds in?" Gunna asked once we were inside of his blacked-out Porsche truck.

"You only get one chance at this shit, Gunna. One time to fuck up. One time to be a little late or come up a little short. One time to make a decision that could cause us all to end up behind the wall or in the fuckin' dirt. I see you in yo' feelings and shit, but this is business; it's not personal. I'd never let a muthafucka put my baby in this position, because when I make moves, it's making sure that everybody that has my last name is goin' to be good regardless of the outcome."

Gunna nodded his head and started up his truck and backed out of Ike's driveway like a bat out of hell. He didn't say anything else, which wasn't like him. I knew that this wasn't the way that he wanted the shit to play out, but this was the way that it had to be. He knew when he called me how I was goin' to handle it. Ike letting his cousin make the trip was goin' to cost him his life, and his cousin would never live to do the time he was going to receive. His cousin got pulled over an hour after leaving Denver; the nigga was drunk and speeding.

Even though I'd get my money to replace my product, I still had other shit to worry about now. Mine and Ike's names were attached to each other from another business, and his cousin was booked under his name. When the fingerprints came back, they'd realize that it wasn't Ike, but they still had his ID, which could fuck with my shit either way it went, depending on whose desk the file went on.

"I'm hungry," Gunna's big ass said, taking me away from my thoughts.

"Nigga, yo' big ass is always hungry. What the fuck is new? It's damn near midnight, and you still tryin' to eat. Take me to my fuckin' car," I spat, not having time to get a full course meal with his big ass right now.

Gunna got bigger every time I saw his ass. He wasn't a big sloppy nigga; he kept himself together. Gunna weighed about 250 and only stood at five feet six. He was the spittin' image of my pops, from their skin to the extra weight. The nigga took five to six showers a day because he had OCD, and he hadn't today, and I could tell because his whole vibe was off. Gunna's hair was all over his head, and his beard was all raggedy lookin'; that's how I knew he was in his feelings. That nigga would pay the barber and Black to come to him to make sure his shit was good.

"All my bitches love my big ass." Gunna bragged but had the right to.

Them dumb ass bitches would do any and everything that this nigga said. Whatever the fuck this nigga was sayin' and doin' to them bitches got 'em hooked fast. Gunna was zooming through the lanes as my phone started vibrating from a voicemail. I read the voicemail preview as soon as it came through as Gunna slammed on his brakes. If I didn't have on a seat belt, I would have gone through the damn windshield.

"So, you stop at this red light, nigga?" I asked, lookin' up from my phone as the muthafuckas on the side of us bass boomin' in their speakers made Gunna's windows rattle.

"Nigga, it's icy as hell out he—" Gunna stopped midsentence.

Lookin' over, I made eye contact with the driver that had his window rolled down. This nigga had fire dancin' in his eyes, and even though I didn't have a clue who the fuck this young ass nigga was, I could see that he wanted me dead. Pullin' my strap from my jeans while not takin' my eyes off this young nigga before he could reach for his strap, I hit him in his head with a bullet as a loud scream started ringin' in my ears. The nigga in the passenger seat was hit right before Gunna sped off into the intersection.

It was only luck that the oncoming traffic didn't crash into us as we made it through the intersection; they slammed on their brakes, just barely missin' us. Gunna was sayin' some shit, but I wasn't even listening. He slowed down his speed as he made his way to the chop shop. Luckily, Ike still lived in the hood. Within minutes, we pulled up to what looked like an auto body shop. Once we were let in the gate, Gunna pulled into the garage as soon as the door lifted.

My mind was runnin', tryin' to figure out who them niggas were. Who would think that they could take me and my brother's life? There were many niggas that when they heard my name, it made them feel a way because of my position. They didn't know the hell that I went through to get to where I was at now. This wasn't some shit that was just put into my lap. I busted my ass to get into this position; it wasn't luck.

Gunna slammed his truck into park and jumped out, still leavin' the truck runnin'. As soon as his feet hit the ground, he pulled out his prepaid cell phone that he used for work purposes. Gunna walked off to talk on the phone, and I jumped out to talk to Bo, who ran the chop shop. Not much needed to be said because I'd been comin' here for years.

"Bo, I need somethin' for a few hours," I said as he looked around at his inventory of cars.

"You a flashy nigga. You just want a ride to the Tesla?" Bo asked in between coughin'.

"Nigga, just get me a fuckin' car," I spat.

I just needed a car that worked. I didn't give a fuck what it looked like. Gunna made his way back over to me as Bo tossed me the keys to a black Impala. I jumped in the driver seat, and Gunna hopped in the passenger seat, and we made our way out. I made my way to a spot that only Gunna and I knew about. I hadn't been to this house in months; I hadn't needed to. I needed to get in the shower and change my clothes before I went home to my daughter.

"Dad!" Amayah screamed from down the hallway.

I didn't respond because her ass was supposed to be gone by now. Her nosy ass heard me walking down the hall. I made my way down the hallway to her room. Every morning, it was the same shit with her; she was always runnin' late. I took a nap after I got in last night, and I was up, so I didn't know what the fuck her excuse is.

"Amayah, why are you still here?" I asked once I made it to her bedroom doorway.

"Dad, can Bri and Tiffany come over tonight after practice?" Amayah asked in between tearing up her room lookin' for somethin'.

"Why do them hoes always have to be at my house?" I asked, walkin' into her room to check her calendar to see if anything important was happening soon.

"Dad." Amayah whined as I made my way out her room.

"You better not be late to school!" I yelled, and she came runnin' out of her room.

"You need to call Black and get yo' dreads re-twisted!" she shot back between laughs.

She looked just like her momma, from her chocolate skin to her long, thick hair. Amayah hugged me tight as I kissed her on her forehead, and she went flyin' down the spiral staircase. She better not get a ticket in that car, or it would be parked. If she didn't stay up all night talkin' to the same hoes she saw every damn day, she wouldn't be running late.

I couldn't complain about Amayah because she got all A's, and in sixteen years, I had never had any bullshit from her. I didn't want her cheerleading, but she loved that shit. All them bitches were hoes, but Amayah knew that I wasn't having that shit. She also played volleyball, and she gave the shit her all, so if it made her happy, then I was all for it.

"Your brother is here." Faith's voice boomed through the intercom on my bedroom wall as soon as I walked in the room.

I snatched up my phone off my nightstand and picked up my iPad to check my estate. Nothin' was out of place, but I'd be lying if I said this life that I chose didn't make me paranoid. Gunna was supposed be finding information about the niggas from last night. He must have had some information, if he was here this early. Every morning, no matter what time I went to sleep, at 4 a.m., I was up. This nigga Gunna might not get up until three or four in the afternoon.

"Wassup," I said as I walked into my kitchen as this nigga made himself at home.

Faith finished cleaning up the kitchen and made her way out. I'd known Faith since we were kids. Faith was family, and she was one of the only people that I trusted with my daughter outside of my family. I used to pay her to babysit my little sister, Honey, so I could hit the block when I first jumped off the porch. Faith worked for me now, full time, taking care of my home and making sure Amayah is good when I wasn't able to.

Gunna was making a big ass plate of the breakfast that Faith had cooked. I hadn't even eaten yet. This nigga was always eating. His eyes were low, and by the way he was walkin', I knew he'd been up all night drinking, smoking, and eating. I knew he was fucked up behind Ike being gone, but right now, he needed to be worried about the muthafuckas that wanted to take us out.

"Nigga, what the fuck did you find out?" I spat as this nigga sat down to eat, like I had invited him over for a meal.

"Damn, relax. I have to eat three meals a day," Gunna replied, pissin' me off.

"Yo' big ass eats way more than three meals a day. Nigga what the fuck did you find out?" I spat, sittin' down.

"The niggas that you hit were some nobodies. Some young niggas named Brad and Joe. But—"

"Somebody else wants our heads," I replied, cuttin' him off.

"Yeah, but it was a pregnant bitch named Gia in the car

with them," Gunna mentioned casually, like that wasn't a fuckin' issue.

"What hospital is she at?" I asked.

I got all the information that I needed, and I went over the plan in my head of how I needed to handle this. My phone started vibrating with a text from Skitzo tellin' me what I already knew—that the job was finished with Ike. I got up and grabbed my plate out of the microwave that Faith had made me. I ate as Gunna and I finished discussin' business.

After about thirty minutes, my phone vibrated, and it was Nana, so I answered.

"Wassup, Nana?"

"Don't fuckin' what's up me. Why yo' black ass haven't been to my damn house? You need to come and take out my damn trash before I turn this muthafucka into a nightmare! I'm sick of Honey, Rose, and Flower. I want them all the fuck out my house. And who the fuck told you to send that bitch over here to clean my house?" Nana rambled.

"Nana, I'm on my way now."

"Answer my damn question. Why the hell would you send that little picked up head girl to my house? Nigga, I ain't never kept no dirty house. What you need to do is talk to yo' dumb ass sister. Her dumb ass couldn't even go to the store for me because that boy got her truck. If you want to send somebody over here to do somethin', send me a bitch that can run to the store."

"Nana, what do you need from the store? I'll go get it before I come."

"If I would have not played my number and it came out, I would have fucked you and ya daughter up."

"Nana, my baby doesn't have nothin' to do with this."

"If I win the megamillions tonight, I'm goin' to lay on somebody's damn beach for a week. What the fuck did I do to deserve y'all sorry ass as family?"

"What beach you want to go to? I can set that up right now."

Chapter Two

MILAN SIMMONS

"Fuckkk!" A man groaned as I walked into the women's bathroom.

"Suck, yo' dick, baby," the same man said as I made my way into an open stall.

I peed as fast as I could and made my way out.

"You like that shit, daddy?" a woman cooed.

"Do that shit just like that," my husband said as I walked over to the sink, causing my heart to fall into my stomach.

I washed my hands and dried them off and turned to leave. I had to get the fuck out of here before I ended up in jail. I couldn't believe what the fuck I was hearing right now. Trying to fight back tears that were forming in my brown eyes because I couldn't let these people see me walk out of here with my makeup running down my face.

"Damn, Jasmine. That's why I love yo' ass," Ervin, my

husband, said, and I slammed the bathroom door and stormed over to the stall they were in.

I kicked the bitch in with all the strength I had. The stall door slammed into the back of Jasmine, knockin' her to the floor. Jasmine might've weighed 110 pounds, if that, so it didn't take much for her to fall. Ervin was a solid 250, so he wouldn't fall as easy.

"This is what the fuck you do to me?" I cried out.

"Baby, wait. Let me explain," Ervin pleaded, stuffin' his dick back in his pants.

"Let you explain that you're lettin' this bitch suck your dick while your wife and her husband are sittin' at the table lookin' like two fuckin' goofies!" I yelled.

"It's not what it looks like," Ervin said, comin' out of the stall as I leaned against the sink.

Jasmine was strugglin' to get off of the floor, and this muthafucka had the nerve to be glancin' back at the bitch. I wished the fuck he would help that bitch up, as she slipped and slid on the urine that was on the floor.

"Don't fuckin' touch me!" I yelled as Ervin tried to grab my hand.

"Look, bitch, he's mine. We've been fuckin' for years. I'm not goin' anywhere. He already had the divorce papers drawn up," Jasmine said as she leaned against the bathroom stall, foldin' her arms across her chest.

From her cheap dress and shoes to her dry clip-ins, I already knew the type of woman she was. She couldn't walk a mile in my shoes if I gave them to her. She probably can't even boil water, so I knew that what I brought to the table, she could never. Knowing the type of man that Ervin was, I could just about imagine the way that he was handling her, and the fact that she was sucking his dick in here said a lot about how he felt about her.

"What the fuck are you talkin' about? Shut the fuck up, Jasmine! Get the fuck out of here!" Ervin spat at her but was still looking at me.

I knew he hadn't drawn up divorce papers because I'd been with this man since I was sixteen. At twenty-three, now there wasn't a bitch walkin' this earth that could tell me anything about him, except the fact that he was fuckin' her.

"Bitch, please," I spat.

"What the fuck is going on in here?" Jeremey asked as he came bustin' in the bathroom.

"Milan, baby. Let's get out of here so we can talk," Ervin pleaded.

"Tell your co-worker what's goin' on," I suggested.

"You're a dirty ass bitch. I don't know where the fuck you're stayin' tonight, but it's not gon' be at my house!" Jeremey, Jasmine's husband, yelled and stormed out the bathroom.

"I'm done," I calmly said, takin' off my wedding ring and throwin' it in his face.

I looked at myself in the mirror and got myself together as Ervin pleaded for me to hear him out. I ignored him and all of his pleas. I hated this dress and only wore it because it looked good with the shoes that Ervin brought me. It fit my body just right and complemented my wide hips. Once I was satisfied with my appearance, I made my way out the bathroom. How did I not know that this was goin' on? This wasn't the first time that he'd been with this bitch; it couldn't have been.

Jeremey was leaning against the wall in tears. His white skin was bright red and was making his freckles pop. I shook my head and made my way to the front of the building, with Ervin still begging and pleading for me to hear him out. He was being honored tonight as the best sports agent of 2019, so he might want to go back in before he missed that.

"Baby, please. We have too much history. We've been together since we were kids. I don't give a fuck about that bitch. You know that I love you, Milan—"

"Can you get my car please?" I said to the valet, ignoring Ervin.

"Baby, please, we can just go home and talk all of this out, Milan. You can't leave me," Ervin begged.

"Your best bet would be to never come home," I said as the valet pulled up with my Chevy Impala.

The valet opened my door, and I handed him twenty dollars and got in my car and sped off, leaving Ervin in my rearview mirror.

How could he do this to me? Why would he do this to me? I was with him when he didn't have anything. Over the years, I'd never once even looked at another man. When I met Ervin, he was so different from me and everyone that I knew. We lived in the projects, and he talked, dressed, and acted white. All the dope boys wanted me, but no, I wanted

Ervin because he was so different, and I knew he would go on to do all of these wonderful things.

Everything that Ervin dreamed about doing, he had done. He was one of the top sports agents in the game. He'd always had a way with his words, and that came in handy over the years. All the players that other agents went above and beyond for breakin' all the rules for, Ervin didn't have to even break a sweat to get them to sign. He was placed on a pedestal damn near like an athlete, but he never gave me a reason to question that he wasn't being loyal.

As I jumped on the highway, the tears that I had made stop started to fall again. I had to pull over on the side of the road because I couldn't even see clearly. The last thing that I needed right now was to wreck my car.

"God, please take this pain I'm feelin' in my chest. Please give me the strength to get through this. I gave this man all of me, and whatever he needed me to be I was. When he was strugglin' fresh out of college and got his first client, I was the one that was there being his secretary, supporting and encouraging him.

I put my dreams on hold to be there and support him. Why was this happening? We were supposed to be forever!" I screamed, hittin' my steering wheel.

After about ten minutes, I pulled myself together so I could drive home. I knew what I had to do wasn't goin' to be easy, but it had to be done. I just hoped for Ervin's sake he stayed far away from me. I wanted to act a fool and embarrass him at that event, but I couldn't embarrass myself. I had too much on the line to let anyone ruin that.

As I made my way home, I tried to wrap my mind around why this had happened. *Did I miss the signs that he had somebody on the side? How long was this going on without me knowing? Does he love her? Was it because she's white so she would look better on his arm because of business?* All these thoughts were coming to my head.

It took me about thirty minutes until I made it home. As I sat in my driveway, I didn't want to go in, but I dragged myself out the car and made my way in. I knew that I couldn't stay here for long, there were too many memories in this house. What if he brought her here and had her in my bed? I pushed my thoughts to the back of my head and came out of my clothes as I came in the front door and laid down on the couch.

———

"Hello," I said, wiping my eyes and sittin' up on the couch.

"Hi, I'm trying to contact Milan Simmons," a man said.

"This is she."

"Hello, Mrs. Simmons. I'm sorry to be callin' you this early. This is Dr. Tiba. I am calling you regarding your sister, Gionna Jenkins. She was brought into University Hospital by ambulance last night. She was involved in a shooting. Gionna gave birth to her daughter, and she isn't taking it well with her daughter's condition. I have tried to contact Lily Jenkins and haven't been able to reach her.

"Right now, she needs some support because the reality is, her daughter might not make it through the morning—"

"I'm on my way," I assured him and got him off the phone.

Checking the time, it was four in the morning. I'd just barely gone to sleep. I jumped in the shower and threw on the clothes that I had laid out for work today. Even though I didn't know if I was goin' to be able to make it there. Me and Gionna hadn't talked in almost a year. I didn't even know that she was pregnant. I made my way out of the house and jumped in my car within twenty minutes.

So many thoughts were runnin' through my mind. I knew the life that my sister lived, so I could only imagine how the fuck this happened. I had offered my sister to come and live with me and leave her mom's house, which wasn't a healthy environment, but she wouldn't. She had always been infatuated with the niggas that got fast money and could take care of her. Gionna knew that I didn't agree with how she was living, and that was why she wouldn't come live with me.

I made it to University Hospital in about thirty minutes. Once I got the information for what room Gionna was in, I made my way up to her room. My stomach was tight, and I didn't know what to expect. I knew what the doctor said about her daughter's condition, but this was a struggle to even be here. The last words my sister said to me were ringing in my ears.

I made my way in the room as I glanced at Gionna and

some nigga and made my way over to my niece. She was in an incubator. Lookin at her fightin' for her life was one of the hardest things that I'd ever had to do. Kids had always been a soft spot for me, and it was hard for me not to care about every kid I came in contact with. My phone started ringing, and I silenced the ringer, not taking my eyes off of my niece.

"Hi, I'm Milan, Gia's sister, and you are?" I said as I walked over to where Gionna and her friend were sittin'.

"It's my friend, Milan. Please do not start with yo' shit today," Gia said, waving me off.

"You smell like twelve. I don't fuck with the police," the nigga smugly replied.

"I'm not twelve," I said, foldin' my arms across my chest as he mugged the fuck out of me.

This nigga had his baseball cap pulled down so far, I couldn't even see his eyes. He was dressed in all black from his head to his toes. He had his hoodie pulled so tight that I could barely see his face. He smelled so damn good that I could smell him from across the room. He was wearing this Creed cologne that I had been tryin' to get Ervin to wear.

"Gia, what are the doctors saying?" I asked, giving my attention to my sister.

"Not right now, Milan," Gia said, waving me off again.

"He is not important. I'm your sister, and I'm asking about your child, Gionna."

"Mrs. Officer, I'm important. You'll never come in contact with another nigga that is as important as me," the man spat, walking up on me, making me back up into the glass doors of the room.

"I'll be back up here, Gia. Keep yo' head up," the man said to Gia but stared down at me and made his way out the room.

"Gia, who the hell was that?" I asked once I slid the door to the room closed that he left open.

Taking in Gia's appearance, I couldn't help but to shake my head. Her hair was all over the place and was as dry as her skin. Gia always took care of herself. Her momma didn't give her much of a choice, because she surely never did. The bags under her eyes showed me that she hadn't had a good night's rest in a while. Her being mixed with Korean and black, if she didn't get it together soon, she'd be lookin' like she was fifty instead of eighteen.

Gionna had always been small, and she didn't gain much weight from the baby. I was sure she wasn't properly taking care of herself. There was no way that you could do that and live the life that she lived. It broke my heart, the type of life that she was going to subject this child to that didn't ask to be here. I knew that now wasn't the time to get into any of that with her.

"I need to go and hit my blunt. I'll be back," Gia said, damn near trembling.

"That's your problem now. You're always worried about the wrong thing," I said, and Gia stormed out the room with fire dancing in her dark, cold, slanted eyes.

My sister was always doin' some stuff that she had no business doin'. She was always mixed up with people that always had her ass right in the middle of their shit. Nothing was ever her fault; she could never take responsibility for her actions. A nurse came into the room to check on the baby.

"Her eyes are open," the nurse said, taking me away from my thoughts.

I jumped up from my seat and ran over to the incubator, and her eyes were open. I tried to call Gia, and the number I had for her was disconnected. I hoped she came back in here soon. The nurse finished checking her vitals and told me that she would be right back. A few minutes passed, and Gia still wasn't back in the room, but the doctor and nurse came rushing into the room, so I backed away from the baby. I sat down in the chair as Ervin tried to call me from his office phone. I ignored his call and sat back in the chair tryin' to relax.

I emailed my supervisor and let him know what was going on with my sister and that I wouldn't be able to come to work today. As much as Gia clearly didn't want to be around me, I didn't really want to be around her either, but she was my sister. I had no choice. We had different mothers but the same father. Our father was killed when I was ten and she was six. Knowing her mother, she wasn't coming here and wasn't goin' to even return the doctor's phone call.

"Are you Milan?" the doctor asked.

"Yes, my sister should be back in here shortly. She needed to get some air," I assured him.

"Okay, I think some air would do her good. I'm Dr. Tiba. We spoke a little earlier. Your niece opened her eyes, and she hasn't done that since she was born. We are going to run some tests and check a few more things out, and then I'll be back in to talk to you and your sister."

"Okay, that sounds good. I'll be here. I took off at work for today, so I'm not goin' anywhere."

I pulled my work phone out of my purse and texted the two clients that I was supposed to meet today to let them know not to come to the office. I was sure at least one of them wasn't goin' to show up anyways. Working with kids could be challenging at times, but I finally loved what I did. I busted my ass to get into my current position. I went from working for the city of Denver, being paid part-time wages but doing full-time work, to being offered a full-time position as a pre-trial case manager, in six months. It hadn't been easy with taking care of a household and husband, but I got it done.

My personal phone dinged, and I looked at the preview, and it was an email from Ervin. I knew that I was going to eventually have to talk to him, but now was not the time. I wasn't ready, and if he knew what was best for him, he'd better stay far away from me until I was ready.

When I finally made it home last night, I drank a whole bottle of Moët, and I was starting to feel it now. I was still sleepy and now hungry. The nurse went and got me a warm blanket, and I reclined in the chair I was sitting in, waiting for my sister to make her way back in here. There wasn't that much weed in the world.

About an hour passed, and I was already sick of these

people coming in and out of this room. My sister still hadn't bought her ass back in here. She needed to get back here; I didn't even have a number for her. My phone started ringing, and it was a number that I didn't know. I answered it while praying it isn't Ervin.

"Hello," I said.

"Are you still at the hospital?" Gionna asked.

"Yes, I'm here. Where the hell are you at, Gia?" I asked, tryin' to whisper but not hiding my attitude.

"Look, I have some business I need to handle! I'll be back!" Gia screamed.

"Your daughter—"

Click.

I tried to call the number back, and now it was goin' straight to voicemail. This bitch just wasn't goin' to ever learn. I took a deep breath and sent Gia text message, tryin' to get her to come back to the hospital. She read my message, but she wasn't responding.

"I'm sorry. I know this probably sounds crazy. If you don't mind me asking, do you know what my niece's name is?" I asked the nurse.

"Her name is Kiara Milan Simmons," the nurse, Brittney, replied.

I nodded my head and decided to take a nap.

Chapter Three

NIGHTMARE

"I don't care whose party it is, Amayah. You're not leaving this house," I said, looking around her damn near empty room.

"But, Dad—" Amayah whined.

"You should have been thinking about that when you wanted to play grand theft auto in the hood," I said, losing my patience, so I made my way out of Amayah's room before she could say anything else.

When we made it to the house after I picked her up this morning, she saw that I had taken everything out of her room but her bed. All the clothes, jewelry, and other bullshit that she loved so much were gone too. She didn't understand that the shit that she had was a privilege, and if she couldn't do what the fuck she was supposed to be doing, then this was how it would be. I was losing my patience, and if I had it my way, her ass wouldn't ever leave this house again.

"I need my laptop to do my homework!" Amayah yelled down the stairs as I made it to the bottom of the spiral staircase.

"Better get some paper and a pencil," I said, and before I could finish, she was stomping her way back to her room.

I was trying to figure out why the hell my sister was still here. I was home now, and she couldn't even do what the hell I asked her to, so I wasn't tryna talk about shit now. It was somethin' that was keeping her ass here, and it wasn't her niece or me.

"You can't just lock her in her room and never let her come out again," Honey claimed as I walked into the living room.

"I don't need no advice on how to raise my daughter," I spat, wishing she would grab up her shit and get the fuck on.

I snatched the remote from her and sat down in my over-sized recliner.

"She's a teenager; she's going to make mistakes, Maurice. But you need to loosen your grip on her because you not letting her go anywhere is exactly why she's acting out now."

"Worry about them bald ass twins. I got mine," I spat because Honey knew better than to come over here questioning me about my daughter.

"Don't talk about my babies," Honey whined.

"I ain't talking about 'em. I'm just reminding you who you

need to be worried about. You don't have no edges, and they can barely put they hair in a ponytail."

"You not gon' be talking about my kids, and I have edges… now."

I didn't give a fuck about her or my bald nieces right now. My only concern was Amayah. She knew how I felt about anyone telling me what I needed to do when it came to my daughter, so she should have just kept her opinions to herself. Now she was in her feelings. She was supposed to be here watching my house and Amayah while I handled business, but she took it upon herself to give Amayah permission to leave and go and hang out, knowing damn well that I wasn't with that shit, but now she wanted to give me some advice.

When the police contacted me about Amayah being arrested for stealing a car when I was leaving the hospital from seeing that bitch Gia, I was confused as hell because that wasn't even somethin' Amayah would do. That was not in her character, but one night with her damn aunt, and all of sudden she ridin' around in stolen cars.

"Alright, you can get the fuck out. I'm home now," I said, and Honey jumped up, snatching up her shit.

I was just waiting for her to say she needed a ride home. She had a truck. A brand-new G-Wagon that Gunna bought her not even a month ago on her birthday. But that bitch wasn't outside, so I knew her broke ass baby daddy was riding around in it, probably with another bitch. I'd never understand how Honey ended up being dumb over a nigga that wasn't ever shit from the beginning.

"Where the fuck is that truck, Honey?" Gunna questioned as he walked into the room with bags of takeout.

"Y'all muthafuckas need to learn how to call before y'all just show up at my house," I spat, not taking my eyes off the TV.

"My niece called me telling me she was hungry. Nigga, all the shit that you've done, and you trippin' with her about this petty shit?" Gunna questioned.

"Nigga, go and have a baby, then you can decide how to raise it," I spat, looking over at Honey repeatedly blow up her baby daddy's phone.

"My baby ain't gon' be no fuckin' it!" Gunna said, flopping down on the couch and screaming Amayah's name.

My siblings were all I had until I had Amayah. I was sixteen when my parents died in a car crash. Me being the oldest, I had to step up and take care of them. At the time, Gunna was fourteen, and Honey was nine. Nobody wanted to take all of us in. My Nana only wanted to take Honey, and lookin' back at it now, I got it. I was bad as hell, and Gunna would follow behind me and do every damn thing that I did. Honey didn't want to be without me and Gunna, so I did what the fuck I had to do.

We were raised to stick together, and I made a promise to myself I would do whatever needed to be done to make sure that we were never separated. An OG, Murda, that lived a few houses down knew the situation, and he came through one night and saw how we were living. He was cool with my pops, so it wasn't weird because, after our parents' funeral, he always came by and checked on us.

I played shit cool like we were good. Truth was, the lights were off, and I was stealing just to be able to make sure that we ate. When he came in the house and saw that we were burning candles, right away he wanted to help in any way that he could. My momma was big on candles, so we had plenty of them bitches. Murda took us to his house for the night, and the next day, the lights were back on, and he filled the cabinets and refrigerator. He paid the taxes on the house up for the year, and that came right on time because they had been sending notices every month about them being behind.

I knew what Murda did, and I knew that I needed to do somethin' to be able to provide for us. Murda didn't want me to be in the game, but after a month of him lookin' out on all the household bills, I told him that either he taught me what I needed to know or I was goin' to go and start fuckin' with this nigga named Bloccc. Bloccc was a hot head and always on some bullshit, so Murda took me under his wing. Ever since then, I jumped off the porch and never looked back.

I never wanted nothin' close to that for my daughter. That was why the fuck I went as hard as I did, to make sure that she has all the opportunities that she has.

"Amayah, go to yo' room. I don't want to see you until the morning," I said, not taking my eyes off the TV.

"Dad!" Amayah whined.

I ignored her as Amayah snatched the Olive Garden bag from Gunna.

"Eat that, and I promise you won't eat nothin' else in this house," I warned her.

"Dad!"

"You heard what I said," I advised her ass.

She thought about it and whispered somethin' to Gunna, handing him back the bag.

"Bye, Honey. Get the fuck out. Go be a mother to your children," I spat as soon as Amayah was out the room.

She started snatchin' up her shit again, she had spread out all over my damn living room, and stormed out like she had a way to get to wherever the fuck she was going.

"Nigga, did Skitzo find that bitch?" I asked.

"Naw, nigga. He has been waiting for that bitch at the hospital. She hasn't come back. Nigga, it's only the light skin, thick bitch been there," Gunna advised me.

"What's goin' on with her baby?"

"Shit, she is breathing on her own is all that I know."

"Time to bring that bitch out," I spat, and Gunna was lookin' at me like I was crazy.

I'm sure that bitch thought staying away from the baby would stop the baby from being in harm's way, but I didn't give a fuck 'bout none of that shit. Just like I told that bitch, I would kill her and her baby. I meant that shit. I gave the bitch word for word what the fuck she was supposed to tell the police, but if the bitch was missing, then she couldn't even talk to the police.

"Nigga, I don't know about kidnapping no fuckin' baby," Gunna admitted with worry sketched all over his face.

"You don't need to worry about shit but findin' that bitch, and then the baby can stay where the fuck she at. So, nigga, you got seventy-two hours. Up the price on that bitch. I need to find that hoe dead or alive at this point!" I got up from my chair and left Gunna standing in the middle of my living room floor.

―――――――――

Ever since Amayah caught her case three weeks ago, she'd been moping around the house like a sad puppy. I didn't give a damn; she should have thought about the consequences before she got in that fuckin' car. I still didn't know her side of what happened, and I was done asking. I knew her ass better get to talkin' before it was time to go to court and before we met with the lawyer about this shit.

"What, is you scared?" I asked Amayah as she put on another coat of fuckin' lip gloss.

"No," Amayah lied, because I knew her ass.

After about twenty minutes, I finally found a parking spot, so we made our way into the building to meet with this pre-trial case manager. Just watching Amayah uncomfortable as hell, I knew that she wasn't built for this shit. She never lived in the hood. Our family was as close to the hood as she had ever gone besides her momma and 'em a few times. I thought until this shit happened, now I'm questioning a bunch of shit. Clearly, she knew more than I thought she did and had some associates that I didn't know shit about.

I rang the bell on the desk because there was no receptionist sitting out here. Amayah was nervous, patting her foot, digging at these expensive ass nails that I was about to make her get taken off. A Mexican man with a bald head and arms covered in tattoos finally came out and asked who we were here to see and then disappeared back into the room filled with cubicles.

A few minutes passed, and Gia's sister came out from the back.

"Hi, I'm Milan, the case manager that has been assigned to Amayah while she is on pretrial," she said as she came into the lobby, extending her hand.

"Hi, I'm Maurice," I said, looking over the woman standing in front of me as I shook her hand, and she turned to greet Amayah.

"We can go in here," Milan said, pointing toward a small conference room that I had peeped from sitting in the lobby since the door was open.

I can't lie; Milan was bad, but she was the police just like I told her ass when I saw her at the hospital. It had been a month since that bitch Gia went missing, and her baby should be getting taken any moment now. I had to postpone taking her because she had so many health problems. Once I got the green light from one of Gunna's bitches that worked at the hospital, I gave the green light to get it done.

When she came out and introduced herself, I damn sure didn't think she was going to say she was the case manager. Maybe the secretary that I still hadn't seen, but not a damn case manager. She was thick in all the right places, caramel skin, pretty face, and her ass was fillin' out the business suit that she was wearing.

She led the way to the conference room. Once we sat down, this bitch wasted no time going over each step of how the pretrial would be for Amayah. I looked across the table at her, to make sure that she was paying attention. I could see her mind running tryin' to take in all the information that this fast talkin' bitch was sayin' so fast that I could barely keep up.

"What's yo' name again? Could you slow down?" I spat.

"Milan. Oh, I'm so sorry. I tend to talk fast," the woman replied and went on to explain everything.

Slowing her ass down, Milan started to relax. From what I knew about Gia, I knew that she was a hoe from the projects, but her sister must've had some money from the ice drippin' from her wrist. I was a little confused to why she was now asking Amayah about her hobbies and things she liked to do. What the fuck did this have to do with her catching a charge for being in a stolen car? Because she was not goin' to cooperate with them and tell them who stole the car, she was being charged with stealing the damn car.

"So, if you could tell me about Amayah at home. Are there any concerns that you have? Anything that you think that she needs to work on?"

"I'm here about this charge Amayah caught. I don't need no muthafuckin advice about how to raise my daughter. All you need to worry about is monitoring her because she isn't goin' to reoffend. As far as my parenting, that don't got shit to do with you."

"Sir, I know that this is a difficult situation to be in, and I know that you probably feel overwhelmed because now several people have been added to the team to ensure Amayah is successful on pretrial and doesn't reoffend. But the reason why I am asking these questions is so that I can get to know you guys better and see what I can do to help—"

"You can't help me with sh—" I attempted to say before Amayah cut me off.

"Dad, chill," Amayah suggested as I gave my attention to her.

"Maybe I should have my supervisor take over if you don't want to answer the questions from me, because unfortunately, we do have to ask these questions," this whore threw out, leaning back in her chair.

"Yeah, get somebody else," I spat, waving my hand, dismissing this bitch.

Milan made her way out the room.

"Dad, why are you trippin'? I like her," Amayah whined.

"Why? Because the bitch got some long ass tracks and some long ghetto ass nails like you? You don't even know this bitch. Everybody ain't yo' friend, Amayah, and you need to learn that. That's why the fuck we are here dealing with this shit now," I said as a black man and Milan came into the room.

"Hi, I'm Mike," the man said. "It seems that you're concerned because of some of the questions that Milan is asking. I'm goin' to be honest with you. All of this is standard. We have to get all of this information to be able to report back to the court. We also need to know what we can put in place to ensure that Amayah is safe in the community.

"From the information that we have, it could simply be a situation where Amayah needs to get some new friends. And if that's the case, then we can proceed from there, but we have to get answers to these questions before we can move forward," Mike insisted.

"Can Amayah have another case manager, because she was talking to her like she tryin' to be friends, and my daughter doesn't need any old ass friends."

"Sir, I assure you that is not the case. I honestly think that she would be the best fit to work with Amayah at this time out of all of the case managers that we currently have."

"We will see about that," I said, tryin' to get this shit over with.

Mike sat in the room with us as Milan went over all the questions that she needed to ask. I still didn't like the friendly bitch, but I needed to get the fuck out of here, so I just went with the shit. After about ten minutes, Mike got a call, so he had to leave out. He gave me his card and told me to call him if we had any issues.

"So, what do you do for a living, Mr. Rogers?" Milan questioned.

"I'm in real estate. Why?"

"I'm asking because I need to know will I need to see about programs that may be able to keep Amayah entertained and out of trouble after school if you're going to be busy with work. Maybe a mentor would be helpful, someone that could take her out and show her positive things in the community, help her look for employment. I know she mentioned wanting a job," Milan suggested.

"As long as it's not you," I said, and she repositioned herself in her chair.

Milan bit on her lip. I knew that she wanted to say more, but she knew better. If for nothin' else, she wanted to keep her job. I just sat back and decided to let her and Amayah talk, because this wasn't my case; it was hers. I never thought that I would be in this position with my baby. Up until now, she never did any wrong in my eyes, and I still saw her as my baby. But now my baby wanted to hang with niggas that wished they could be me.

"Okay, so if you have any questions, you can call me or text me, Mr. Rogers," Milan said, handing me her card.

"Text you? How fuckin' professional is that?" I questioned.

"Well, Mr. Rogers, I have a lot of clients, and sometimes it's more convenient for me and other clients to text to communicate. If that doesn't work for you, please feel free to call me."

"You can cut the Mr. Rogers shit. I ain't ya fuckin' grandpa. Call me Maurice," I said, getting up from the table.

Milan didn't have anything else to say, and neither the fuck did I, so we made our way next door so Amayah could take the drug test that they claimed was mandatory, even though this wasn't no fuckin' drug case.

"Dad, I gotta tell you somethin'," Amayah said, making me stop in my tracks.

I turned around to look at her, and without her sayin' anything, I already knew what the fuck she wanted to say. Her ass had been smoking. I didn't say shit; I turned around and kept walking as she took her slow, sweet, precious time as I held open the door for her.

"You been smoking crack or playin' wit yo' nose?" I whispered once she got to the door.

"No, why would you ask me that?" Amayah questioned, scrunching up her face.

"Well, I need to know am I raising Bobby Kristina or not. Bring yo' ass on," I said, and we made our way next door.

Chapter Four

MILAN

"**H**ey, Milan, your husband is here," my co-worker Maria said, peeking her head in my office.

"Okay, thanks, girl," I replied and rolled my eyes as soon as she was gone.

This muthafucka just would not leave me alone. I would never tell any of these people here my personal business. On my second day here, I had to shadow Maria, and she told me all about her husband having an affair on her. With her being Mexican, I was so shocked that she was sharing her business with a complete stranger. She told everything that she could think of. I left here and had to have a drink for her, because she had stressed me out with her issues.

As I updated my notes for the clients that I had seen this morning, I couldn't help but to think about Maurice, Amayah's dad. He was definitely goin' to be a handful while

Amayah was on my caseload. He seemed to be pretty confident that her case was goin' to be thrown out; how he had come to that conclusion, I didn't know. Because from the information that I gathered from the police report, she seemed to have been caught red-handed. On paper, she seemed to be a really good kid, but I'd seen crazier things, so I'd just have to wait to see how things panned out.

I could tell by the way that Maurice walked and talked that he was the type of man that got shit done, so he might've had something in motion with their attorney. He had to be the rudest man that I'd ever encountered, but I'd be lyin' if I said that God didn't take his time when He made him. He was the finest man that I'd ever laid my eyes on. I could see that there was more to him than met the eye from the darkness and coldness in his dark brown eyes. His long, neat, and well-groomed dreads and beard with goatee all fit him just right. From his smooth, light skin to his tattoos that covered every part of his arms that I could see from the t-shirt that he was wearing, his body was toned well, and whatever girl that was in his life was definitely lucky.

I made my way out of my office after a few minutes. I was so glad that she did not bring Ervin's ass back here. With her crazy ass husband showing up here once a week, I was sure she was against all men.

"Why are you here, Ervin?" I whispered.

"Can we please just talk?" he pleaded, tryin' to hand me flowers and a bag from Nordstrom's.

"Let's go outside," I said as he tried to hand me that bull-shit again.

I hit the button for the elevator, and it came up faster than usual. We got on, and the tension filled the elevator. I looked straight ahead, and Ervin just stared at me with this puppy dog face that his ass could keep. I watched my momma get cheated on by my dad for years, and the only thing that stopped it was him being murdered. I refused to let any man disrespect me like that. If you cheated once, you'd cheat again, and I wasn't taking any chances with this poor excuse for a man.

As we stepped off the elevator, I saw one of my clients being brought in, in handcuffs. When she saw me, she dropped her head and looked at the floor until she disappeared into intake. Once Ervin and I were outside and away from the building I worked in, he finally spoke.

"Look, Milan. I know that you're upset, and I get that. I want to work this out. I know that it isn't goin' to be easy, but you're my wife. That has to still mean something, right?"

"Did it mean anything when you fucked my sister and got her pregnant?" I asked.

"What? What are you talkin' about?" Ervin asked, slightly twistin' his lips to the left.

"Lying isn't goin' to get us anywhere for sure, now is it? I saw Kiara Milan Simmons' birth certificate. Whose idea was that, yours or hers?" I asked, folding my arms over my chest.

"Look, baby, I can—"

"You can what, explain? Please do."

"That's not my baby, but I did one time."

"One time what, Ervin?"

"Look, it doesn't mean anything. Please, can we go home and talk about all of this, Milan?"

"Just be ready to talk to my lawyer when he calls, because we don't have anything to talk about. I had all of your shit sent to the condo downtown, so you can take it to the projects with Gia or to wherever you and that bitch Jasmine are sleeping," I said and left him standing there with his mouth wide open.

My phone started ringing as I made my way back into work. It was the hospital, so I answered.

"Hello, this is Detective Jones. I'm trying to contact Milan Simmons."

"This is she; how can I help you, Detective?"

"I'm contacting you because I can't seem to contact your sister Gionna Jenkins."

"I haven't been able to contact her either in some time."

"Well, Mrs. Simmons, I'm sorry to tell you this, but it looks like your niece has been kidnapped from the hospital. Something was goin' on with the camera system at the time, and—"

"What the hell do you mean that she's been kidnapped?" I screamed, stoppin' in my tracks.

"Ma'am, I know that this is hard to process. We are doing everything in our power to get to the bottom of this. We have the father listed as Ervin Simmons. Do you know a way that we can contact him? I show here that he signed the birth certificate."

"Yes, I know how to contact him. He's my fuckin' husband!" I screamed, walking away from my job.

"Oh, I'm sorry. I wasn't aware of that, ma'am," the detective assured me.

When the nurse told me that Kiara's last name was Simmons, I didn't think anything of it. My sister got around, and shit, it could have been several niggas that could've been her father as far as I was concerned. But I knew that she was Ervin's child when the same nurse came in the room asking me did I know how to contact Ervin Simmons and confirmed his address with me after I gave it to her. I knew she wasn't supposed to, but she did.

"Can I please have your husband's phone number?" the detective asked after a few minutes of awkward silence.

I gave him the number and hung up on his ass.

"I'm so sorry that this happened, Mrs. Simmons. We are doing everything that we can to find your niece. We have a social worker here that is willing to talk to you if you need to talk to someone. I know that this can't be easy to deal with," Brittney, the nurse, said, tryin' to comfort me as I sat in Kiara's room.

"I'm fine. I have talked to enough people for today," I assured her as my work phone started ringing; it was Amayah.

It had been two weeks, and they hadn't found my niece. I hadn't been able to find her momma, and I was starting to worry that neither of them were coming back.

"Hey, sweetie, is everything okay? It's late; you should be sleep," I said as I answered the phone.

"No," she said in between sniffling.

"What is wrong?"

"Some girl was taggin' Jaleel in pictures of them together all day!" Amayah cried out.

"Sweetie, I know that you don't want to hear this, but—"

"Why would he do this? I was just with him yesterday, and he was sayin' that he loved me. He came to the game and everything. All week he has been coming to my school and bringing me food for lunch. When I come out of practice, he is waiting for me in the parking lot. He texts me back and forth all day while I'm in school..."

I just listened because I knew right now that was all that she wanted. My gut was telling me that it was the Jaleel that was on my caseload and then went on the run right before Amayah caught her case. I knew that he had to be the one that stole the car that Amayah was now being charged for. I was not surprised that he would do her like that; he flipped on his big homie with the case that I was supervising him on. Then he wanted to change his story and was saying that his big homie had nothin' to do with the drugs and gun he was caught with. Then next thing I knew, his grandma was calling me saying that he cut off his ankle monitor and left her home.

Once a client went on the run, I usually just let the police do their job and find them. I had made exceptions for some clients, but I could tell that Jaleel was full of shit, and I hadn't done anything but answer his grandmother's calls. She was worried about somebody doing somethin' to her to get revenge for Jaleel snitchin'. He didn't give a statement in court, but the information that he gave did lead to several arrests and raids, so I was sure his other gang members weren't too happy. The fucked-up thing was I couldn't even guarantee his grandmother her safety. When he was willing to cooperate, they were willing to dedicate an officer in an unmarked car to be on their block, but once he went AWOL, so did that.

As Amayah went on and on about all the empty promises that he made to her, I could hear the hurt and pain in her voice. I knew that there wasn't anything that I could say that was going to make her feel any better. Shit, she hadn't given me any time to even say anything. She just kept going and going. She'd get through this, but I just hoped that this didn't make her fall off from all the good things that she had going for herself.

"Hold on," Amayah whispered.

"Yes, Fay-Fay, I'm in here! I'm good. Coach got us food after practice," Amayah lied.

She just told me she didn't want to eat and couldn't sleep. I hated when kids put me in these positions, not wanting to tell their parents about what was really going on. Amayah's dad didn't want her to do anything or feeling any way that wasn't ran by him first. He was one of those parents that would put a damn chip in her so he could keep tabs.

"Who is Fay-Fay?" Your dad's girlfriend?" I asked.

"Naw, she's like his sister. They grew up together; she's my god mom. Her and my mom used to be best friends. She takes care of our home and looks out for me."

"Oh, okay," I replied.

Not that it was any of my business, but I was curious if he had a girl. Shit, he was fine, and I was sure it was somebody out there that thought she was his girl. I know how females could get at times.

Amayah talked to me about everything under the sun but had never mentioned anything about her dad's love life. At first, I thought that might be the reason that she was rebelling with this boy, but I think that it was because of the on-again, off-again relationship with her mom. She never had anything good to say about her mom, but I could tell that she was still waiting for her mother to be the mom that she always wanted. The sad thing was I didn't think that she would ever get that, well at least not from her.

"Sweetie, you really need to try to eat something and get some rest. You have school in the morning, and it's almost two."

"I know. I'm goin' to go to sleep, and I'll eat in the morning before I go to school," Amayah replied.

"Okay, get some sleep. If you need to talk tomorrow, just call me. Do not call Jaleel," I threw in.

"I'm not calling him. I never call or text him first, and I'm not going to start now," Amayah insisted. "I have a cheer-leading competition that starts Friday. Is there any way that you can come? It's after business hours."

"I can try to. I'll let you know as soon as I know for sure. I have a lot of stuff on my plate right now."

We said our goodbyes and ended the call. I got up to leave as a nurse came in to check on me. I said my goodbyes, and she assured me that she would personally call me if she heard anything about my niece/stepdaughter's whereabouts. I made my way home because my head was starting to hurt. As I made my way out the hospital, I was stopped by two white men in suits.

"Are you Milan Simmons?" one of the men asked.

"Yes, and you are?"

"I am Federal Agent Clark, and this is Agent Burns. Is there any way that we can get a moment of your time?"

"Is this regarding my niece?" I asked.

"No, unfortunately it's not. This is about one of your clients' father. We have tried to contact you at your home, but we haven't been able to. I understand with what you're going through with your niece why you have been hard to get in contact with. We tried to reach you at work, but they advised us that you had left early today."

I stepped away from the entrance because we were blocking people from being able to get in and out of the doors.

"Any information that I have regarding my clients' parents

would be in their file, which I'm sure my supervisor could give you."

"We have been given information that leads us to believe that you may know more than is in the file about Amayah Rogers' father, Maurice Rogers. We have seen you meeting her at school and even completing home visits," Detective Clark advised me.

"That is all a part of my job, and all of that information is in the file. I'm sorry, I'm not sure what other information it is that I can give you. Amayah is my client; I don't know much about her father."

"Is it a part of your job description to take Amayah to get her nails done and shopping at the mall? I mean, let's be honest, Mrs. Simmons, she was arrested for auto theft. What are you doing rewarding her?" Detective Burns questioned.

"If you have any other questions then you need to contact my lawyer, because at this point, you are disrespecting me," I said and walked away leaving dumb and dumber standing there.

I made my way to my car as my phone started ringing, and it was a number that I didn't recognize, so I sent it to the voicemail. I got into my car and started making my way home. Lately, I hadn't been wanting to even go home. I had to start looking for somewhere else to stay, but I didn't know when I'd find the time to do that.

After about twenty minutes, I made it home, but after sitting in my car and thinking for about ten minutes, I decided to not go in just yet. Backing out of my driveway, my mind started to race wondering if I was doing the right thing. It was on my heart, and I was not going to be able to sleep until I did it.

I arrived at my location. After I was interrogated by the man at the gate, he let me into the estate. I'd only been here twice, but each time, I was blown away by this beautiful home that Amayah had. I wish I'd grown up in a place like this. I had become so invested in getting her back on the right track because I saw so much potential in her.

"What the fuck are you doing at my home this time of night?" Maurice spat as I got out of my car.

"I needed to talk to you," I said, turnin' tryin' to stop the wind from hittin' me in my face.

"About what? Because business hours are between eight to five Monday through Friday. Amayah ain't did nothin' she not supposed to do," he spat.

"Look, I shouldn't even be telling you this, but I know how much you mean to Amayah, and with her mother not being around consistently, you are all she has as far as parents. I just was approached by two federal agents, and they were tryin' to find out what I knew about you and—"

"Alright," he said, cuttin' me off.

"I know that you talk yo' shit and think that I'm the police and this and that, but I'm not. Being from where I'm from, I can't believe that I'm even in the position that I'm in with the city. I really just care about the best interest of Amayah, and that is the only reason why I'm coming to you with this," I pleaded.

He just stared at me but hadn't said anything. He slipped his hands into the black Nike sweats that he was wearing as my eyes traveled down the jogging suit that he was wearing and landed on his dick.

"I'm goin' to go now," I said, turnin' to leave.

"Do yo' nigga know where you at? He let you come out and make house visits this late at night? Or are you strapped?"

"I don't have a man," I admitted for the first time out loud.

"Mrs. Officer, make sure you have yo' ass at my baby's cheer competition Friday," he said as I got in my car.

Chapter Five

NIGHTMARE

I watched as Amayah did her hair. She hadn't said anything to me since last night when I told her that she couldn't drive her car. I gave Faith the day off. I hated Amayah wasn't talkin' to me. Anybody else, I wouldn't give a fuck, but my baby—this shit was fuckin' with me. We had never been through this shit before, and it had only been a few hours that she'd even been awake.

"How long you gon' do this not talkin' to me shit?" I asked.

"Why do you care? I should just go and live with my mom so that girl can be over here," Amayah stated, like she knew it was the truth.

"You know me better than that. I do care about you, but this bullshit with this car got me tight. I'm not gon' lie to you. I'd buy you the fuckin' world if I could. You haven't ever asked for somethin' and didn't get it. I'm just tryin' to figure out when did you stop coming to me about what the fuck is goin' on with you.

"What you doin' talking to ya momma? If somethin' is goin' on with you, you need to be talking to me first. And you'll go and live with Gunna if somethin' happens to me."

"Uncle Gunna's? He doesn't even have no furniture," Amayah said in between laughing.

"Well take that sleeping bag that you begged me for and only used in the damn living room," I said, making Amayah laugh.

"Dad, I was ten, and that's because you never let me go anywhere," Amayah said, looking at me for the first time in the mirror of her vanity in her bathroom.

"Finish getting ready so that I can take you to see ya momma," I said, tappin' the wall and making my way through her room and down the stairs.

I didn't hate many people, but I hated my baby momma, Nadia. I didn't give a fuck about her and me not workin' out. I just hated the way she did my daughter. She came in and out of her life when it was convenient for her. That shit wasn't fair to Amayah, and even though she never talked about it, I knew that shit bothered her. I could tell by how she acted whenever she came back from fake ass spending time with her. Nadia hadn't even seen Amayah in four months and twenty-five days to be exact.

Amayah had that shit written down on her calendar in her room. I checked it every so often so I can make sure I was on top of important shit that might slip my mind. When I looked at her calendar today, I knocked the bitch off the tack that was holdin' it on the wall, and it flipped open to the last day she'd seen Nadia. That shit made me flip through the calendar so I could see if she always wrote that shit down, and she did.

After about twenty minutes passed, Amayah made her way into the living room dressed like she was in the feds. I started laughin' so damn hard that my stomach started hurtin'.

"What's so funny?" Amayah asked with an attitude.

"Nothin, baby. You ready?"

"Dad, shut up. I know why you're laughin'. I look like a bum. You took all of my clothes. Why do I have to wear this?" Amayah whined, stompin' her feet.

"Girl, we goin' to the hood, not a fashion show. Shit, you'll fit right in," I said, getting up from my chair.

Amayah pouted as I draped my arm over her shoulder, and we made our way out. Once we were in the truck on the road, Amayah didn't say much. Shit, my mind was on Nadia's funky, trifling ass. She'd better have her ass at her momma's like she told Amayah she would be. Amayah snatched my phone out of the holder on the dashboard. Amayah changed the song and put my phone back in its proper place. It took about forty-five minutes until we made it to our destination.

"Inmate, we here," I said as I pulled on to Nadia's momma's place.

"That's why you were laughin'? I look like them pictures on Facebook and IG when girls be sayin' they are practicing their jail poses," Amayah said, pokin' out her lip as I put my truck in park.

"I don't know what them hoes be lookin' like, but you look just like them girls on Netflix in that show *Girls Incarcerated* that you had me watching."

"Whatever, dad. I'll call you when I'm ready," Amayah said as she went to open the door, but I stopped her.

"Is yo' momma even here? Because I'm not leavin' if she ain't. I don't even see her car," I said, looking up and down the block for Nadia's car.

"She doesn't have that car anymore," Nadia said, looking out the window.

I handed her my phone, not sayin' a word, so she could call her momma. I could hear it ring, and with each ring, Amayah impatiently tapped her foot waiting for Nadia to answer. She ended the call and then called her right back, and still no answer. The pain that I saw every time Nadia let her down started to show all over Amayah's face.

"She's coming. She's on her way. We can just wait for her to get here," Amayah protested.

For my daughter's sake, that bitch better be on her way. I turned up this Lil' Baby nigga that I hated, but I knew that Amayah loved his ass. As he boomed through my speakers, I started rapping along, and Amayah looked at me crazy and snatched my phone out the holder. I knew her ass was recording me, but I kept goin' as long as it made her smile.

Amayah started to rap along and flipped the camera on her as she rapped along to every word this nigga was sayin'. I stopped and let back my seat to try to get comfortable, because I knew that this bitch wasn't coming. Because Amayah wanted to wait, I'd wait, and only for her. Amayah rapped and recorded videos of herself on my phone for what felt like forever. I was tryin' not to fall asleep since a nigga only got to take a nap this morning before I had to get up, do my morning ritual, and tend to business.

Checking the time, an hour had passed, and I looked over at Amayah as the music stopped. She tried to call her sorry ass momma as nosy ass Elma made her way out on her porch.

"Y'all can come in. Y'all don't have to sit out there!" Elma screamed from her porch, sounding like she'd smoked a pack of cigarettes every day of her life since she was seven.

I rolled down the passenger side window so she could hear me.

"We good, Elma. You got roaches. I make Amayah throw away whatever she got on whenever she leaves from over here. I ain't takin' none of yo' pets in my shit, Elma Jean!" I yelled so her old ass could hear me as Amayah begged me to stop.

"Fuck you!" Elma yelled, stickin' up her finger and going back into her house, slamming the door.

"Dad!" Amayah whined.

"What? Am I lying?" I asked, and we both started laughin'.

My phone started ringing, and it was Honey. Amayah answered since she was holding onto that bitch for dear life, like she was having iPhone withdrawals. I looked over, and Nana was on the screen, waving.

"Alright, I said hi. Maurice, ya black ass need to call me

the regular way. You know I don't do all this shit. The feds probably watchin' this shit, and I don't want them coming to get me. I'm too damn old to go to jail. Big Bertha ain't gon' be fuckin' with me," Nana said, and the screen went black.

"Nana is crazy," Amayah struggled to say in between laughing.

"Hun, girl, take this damn phone. Amayah think she damn Bonnie ridin' around with a broke ass Clyde and done got caught. Hun, y'all all gon' end up in jail, and I can tell you who ain't goin'. I ain't goin'!" Nana said as Honey came onto the screen.

Amayah didn't think that shit was funny, and her whole attitude changed. I looked over, and Don, Nadia's brother, brought his weird ass out on the porch to smoke a cigarette. One minute this nigga a deacon at some church, the next thing I knew, he was at one of my spots tryin' to sell shit that he had stolen, tryin' to get high. Don was forty and still living at home with his momma. Had a whole bitch and three kids, and they all lived in this house too. Nadia's people didn't fuck with me because me and Nadia weren't together, and I didn't give a fuck either way, because they wasn't nothin' but a bunch of bums.

Honey and Amayah talked, and from hearing Honey's voice, I knew that something was goin' on with her. When we left from over here, I'd go over there and check on her and Nana. Amayah talked to Honey for a few minutes, and then Honey told her she would call her back. Time was flying by, and before I knew it, another hour had passed, and Amayah was just staring out the window. She even turned off the music.

"Daddy, we can go," Amayah said, not even looking over at me.

I didn't say anything; I just sat up and started up the car and pulled away.

"Amayah, I get it. I know that you want your mom to be in your life. I know that as a man, it's some shit that I can't teach you about being a woman. But fuck—"

"Dad, I don't want to talk about it right now," Amayah finally said, turning to me with a face full of tears.

I pulled out my phone and found the number I was lookin' for and pressed call.

"Where you at?" I asked once the call connected.

"Excuse me?"

"Girl, where the fuck are you at?"

Beep, beep.

I knew this bitch didn't hang up on me. My phone started vibrating, and after lookin' at the number, I didn't recognize it. I answered.

"Leaving my lawyer's office downtown off of sixteenth, Maurice."

"Meet us at The Cheesecake Factory," I said and ended the call.

"Dad, I can't go nowhere lookin' like this," Amayah whined.

"Then stay in the car. Faith went and got that peanut butter that you like for the peanut butter and jelly sandwiches, because I know your ass is sick of noodles. The way I see it, you might want to come in here and eat because when we get home, you're back to eating like an inmate," I said, making my way to the cheesecake factory.

Amayah rolled her eyes and started checkin' herself out in the visor mirror.

My phone started ringing, and Amayah snatched it out the holder like it was somebody callin' for her.

"Uughh! Kay is so annoying. I never even seen her, and she gets on my nerves," Amayah said, puttin' my phone back in the holder.

"She is," I said, making Amayah laugh.

Kay knew what it was and what it will always be between us. I called the bitch when I wanted to fuck, nothin' more and nothin' less. We didn't go on dates; we didn't even chill before we fucked. She got her nut, I got mine, and I made my way home.

She thought because she got regular dick that it was eventually goin' to be more, but it wasn't. How we started was exactly how we were goin' to finish. She was always tryin' to be more than what we are.

She was always offering to do shit for my daughter and this and that. That was why I paid Faith; I didn't need no bitch thinkin' that she was playin' momma to my daughter. Because as soon as a bitch fixed her mouth to say somethin' to my baby, she'd be getting beat the fuck up. Not by me, but I'd definitely pay somebody to do it.

It took about five minutes, and we made it to our destination. I found a parking spot not too far away.

"Who comin' to meet us?" Amayah asked.

"You'll see in a minute," I replied.

"Well, at least I know it ain't Kay. Why don't you ever bring her around?" Amayah asked as I got out of the truck.

I didn't respond; I made my way over to open her door. My daughter had never been around no woman outside of my blood family except Faith, so I didn't know why she was even askin' about Kay. The only reason why she even knew that Kay existed was because she was so damn nosy, and Honey be tryin' to tell my business that she didn't know shit about.

As we made our way to the restaurant, Amayah was walkin' with her head down. I grabbed her hand, and she still was lookin' at the dirty ass sidewalk, pissin' me off.

"Amayah J'ene Rogers, put yo' muthafuckin' head up," I said as calmly as I could, and she quickly looked up at me.

"Baby, unfortunately muthafuckas are goin' to let you down, but you already know I don't play that shit. She's missin' out because I raised a smart, beautiful car thief. I've never talked down on yo' momma to you, and I'm not goin' to start, but never let nobody make you feel a way because of the decisions that they make.

"Even lookin' like an inmate, you never let nobody outside of my people know that somethin' is goin' on. You could be ugly like Elma Jean. You need to count yo' blessings. You goin' to church with Nana on Sunday," I said as we made it on the side of the street the restaurant is on.

"Daad—" Amayah said and let go of my hand and ran over to Milan once she noticed her standing by the restaurant.

"This is my baby," I reminded her once I got to where they were.

"Maurice, all my clients feel the same way about me that Amayah does. I'm not tryin' to steal your baby. You invited me here," Milan said as Amayah clung to her.

"You just needed to be reminded so you can make sure you stay in yo' place," I said, holding open the door so they could go in the restaurant.

"My place, hun?" Milan asked as we made our way to the hostess.

The hostess led the way to the table as I watched Milan's ass bounce in the Nike jogging suit she was wearing. Her ass was one that a nigga could never forget if I tried. It was not too big but just right. I was up for hours tryin' to figure out why she came to me after the feds paid her a visit. I called my lawyer, lettin' him know, and I still couldn't sleep. I was tryin' to figure out why she cared so much about Amayah that she would put her job on the line to still try to protect her.

She damn sure wasn't tryin' to protect me. When Amayah got in the booth with her, I looked at her crazy, and her eyes got big.

"Dad, Milan is single, and she would be perfect for you. You must like her because you invited her here," Amayah sang, tryin' to smooth things over.

"She's here because I knew that you would be happy to see

her. You know she's the police. That's the only reason she's sittin' at the table with us."

"Maurice, I'm not, and if you knew me then you would know that," Milan threw in.

"Dad, she's really not. She's so cool, and she doesn't even like the police. Just like you. She loves football just like you. She loves Mob movies, old school cars, seafood, and you do too," Amayah pleaded as the waitress took our drink orders.

I didn't respond because I'd been hearing all this shit since Amayah started talkin' to her every day. I knew that Amayah was clinging to her because of the situation with her mom. I knew there was nothin' that I could buy or do that would ever take away the fact that Nadia wasn't shit, so that was why I stopped trippin' about how much time they spent together. I didn't like it, and I had one of my workers close by whenever they were with each other. I also put a keychain on Amayah's wallet that recorded their conversations.

I would take it off as soon as she got back home. My baby was raised, even though she didn't know, to follow the G-code. She said just enough, but never too much, to keep you guessing to everybody. Even though she fucked with Milan hard, I always could tell by the tone change in her voice that she knew at the end of the day where her loyalty was, and that was with me.

Chapter Six

MILAN

"I'll be right back," Amayah said as she damn near ran to the bathroom.

"When's the last time you been with a real nigga?" Maurice asked as soon as Amayah disappeared from his sight.

"What?" I asked.

He didn't say anything but waited for my response.

"To be honest, I haven't," I admitted.

When my lawyer told me that the private investigator found out some disturbing information about Ervin, I was so hurt and confused. I could feel my heart breaking more than it already was. Then Maurice called before I could even let the reality of my life set in. I didn't even put up a fight; I just came to meet him here, not knowing that Amayah was even going to be here. I needed to get away from my problems, even if it was only temporary.

"I know, I can tell. I just wanted to see if you were goin' to lie," Maurice admitted.

A few seconds passed with Maurice lookin' at me like he was examining me. Just staring at his lips, I just wanted to kiss 'em, but I knew that was because I was hurt and just wanted somebody to take the pain away, even if it was temporary. From that print in his pants, I knew that he could get the job done with ease.

"Why would you risk all that you got goin' on for Amayah?" Maurice asked as I took a sip of my drink.

"I do what I do for a living because I love kids. I know what it's like to not have a voice and not have anybody that understands, or hell, care about what you're goin' through. That is why I go above and beyond for all the kids that I work with. I spend extra time with Amayah that's off the clock because I know what it feels like to have a mother in the same city with you and doesn't even bother to pick up the phone to call you on your birthday."

He didn't say anything because I knew that he knew where I was coming from. Even with the silence that lingered between us, I knew that he was taking everything in. The waitress came over to the table, placing the appetizer down. Maurice ordered for him and Amayah because I was undecided. Then the waiter took my order and hurried away.

"Does your nigga know where you're at?" Maurice asked.

"I don't have one," I replied as Ervin walked up on the table.

"I thought that was you. How are you doing, Milan?"

Ervin asked as Jeremy, his colleague, continued to follow the hostess.

"I'm doing wonderful," I replied, and he said his goodbyes and walked away.

"How many times you fucked that lame ass nigga?" Maurice asked as Amayah came up on the table.

"So, Dad, you like her more now, huh" Amayah asked as Maurice grilled me, waiting for me to answer his question.

"Girl, be happy you not eating peanut butter and jelly, because after this, that's what you'll be eating," Maurice said in between getting a stuffed mushroom.

"Milan, have you heard anything about your niece yet?" Amayah asked.

"No, unfortunately I'm just waiting."

"What's goin' on with your niece?" Maurice asked, and I caught him up with what had been goin' on.

They brought us our entrées, and as we ate, Maurice continued to talk his shit. Amayah told me about what happened with her mom, and my heart ached for her. I knew what it felt like to have your mother let you down time and time again. If it wasn't for my aunt, I wouldn't know what love was coming from a mother-like figure. Amayah had an aunt that was around a lot, but she was dealing with her own issues. I knew that, no matter what, nobody could ever take away that void of not having your mother in your life.

"I hope you got some of that police money, Mrs. Officer, because I don't buy women that ain't mine meals," Maurice said, cuttin' me off from replying to one of Amayah's many questions.

"Daaad!" Amayah whined.

"I do. I can pay for all of us if you like," I replied.

"Naw, I got me and my baby," Maurice said in between laughin'. "Nobody pays or bring anything to the table for me and mine. Nobody will ever be able to fix their mouth to say they did anything for us."

Amayah rolled her eyes as I put down the money for my bill, and Maurice followed suit. Amayah was layin' it on thick tryin' to convince her dad that I was what he needed. He hadn't said anything, and she just kept on goin'.

"Did you give her enough for your tip?" Maurice asked as I put on my jacket.

"Yes, Maurice."

We made our way out the restaurant, and they walked me to my car. Maurice walked close to the street, and we were on his side. He was doing something on his phone as me and Amayah talked. I knew that he was in construction as well as real estate because I'd done my research, but the visit from the feds had me wondering what else he was involved in. I was up half the night thinking about the possibilities of his lifestyle, while thinkin' about how good he smelled every time I was in his presence.

"Dad, open her door!" Amayah demanded as I hit the locks on my car.

I hugged Amayah and said my goodbyes, walking ahead of them. Before I could grab the door handle, Maurice beat me to it and opened the door. I looked back at Amayah who was by my trunk, cheesin' so hard I couldn't help but smile too.

"I know you want to sit on it because you keep lookin' at it, Mrs. Officer," Maurice said low enough for only me to hear.

"Bye, Maurice," I said, laughin' in between and embarrassed he caught me lookin' at his dick.

"You better be at the competition on Friday," Maurice said and shut my car door.

My phone vibrated, and I knew in my heart it was Ervin, so I sent him to the voicemail and made my way to meet with my realtor.

It took me about thirty minutes to make it to the home that my realtor was showing me today. As soon as I put my car in park, my work phone vibrated, and I tried to ignore, but it kept buzzing, so I answered it, even though I was supposed to be off today. I had taken today off a while ago because it was me and Ervin's wedding anniversary. We were supposed to go to Vegas for a few days. I was goin' to go to work, but I decided to take the time off to find a new place.

"Girl, you're not goin' to believe this. They found Jaleel, and they released him on GPS again," Maria advised me.

"Are you serious?" I asked, not believing what I just heard.

"Yes, girl, they did."

Maria caught me up on Jaleel. I couldn't believe that they would let him out. He didn't have a gun or any drugs on him this time, so that was enough for them to give him another chance. Maria took this shit too personal; that was why she stayed stressin', and her hair was fallin' out. A lot of people that worked in this field didn't really give a fuck about the kids, and they'd be happy if they all could just be locked up forever. I got Maria off the phone because my accountant was calling my phone.

"Hello," I said as I answered Tommy's call.

"Hello, Mrs. Simmons. I wanted to let you know that it looks like a large sum of money has been removed from your joint account with Ervin."

"How much?" I asked, tryin' to stay calm.

"He has wiped out the savings, and you have about five hundred in checking."

"He just made the withdrawal?" I asked, already knowin' the answer.

"Yes, I wanted to let you know because I know that you were planning on using some of those funds for the down payment for a new home."

I took in what Tommy was saying and ended the call. I knew that there was a chance that things were about to get messy, but I never thought he would go to this extreme. He was clearly in his feelings because he'd seen me with Maurice.

I pulled myself together and finished waiting for my realtor to get here. Ervin was the type that had to get his way by any means necessary. He was used to being able to buy his way into whatever he wanted since he had money at his disposal. So I wasn't even surprised that he was tryin' to use money to get his way.

I knew that Ervin was going to show his ass today. After him pullin' that shit with the joint account, I didn't know why he would show up here at the house. I don't want to talk to him, let alone see him, with the information that I was given about him.

I got up to let Ervin in as he banged on the front door and was just layin' on the doorbell. I could see him from the cameras. I knew that he would go to drastic measures when he saw me with Maurice earlier today, but I never thought he would try to use money as leverage. He'd never been that type of man.

He was always a giving man; he would give me his last when he was broke, so when he got money, his giving just grew. I never had to pay bills, and every check I ever got, I saved most of it. My money was in a separate bank account that his name wasn't on. So, he knew that I had my own money, but he had always said his money was ours. Now I guess that had changed because he decided to cheat.

"So, you went and got some thug ass nigga, so you don't need me anymore. What about our history? I love you. Don't you love me?" Ervin asked as he came storming into the house.

"Were you thinking about our history when you got with a white woman, had a baby, and moved her around the corner?" I asked after I finished my glass of wine.

"What? I don't know what you're talkin' about!"

I walked over to my bookshelf and pulled out the manila envelope that my lawyer gave me, filled with pictures and receipts of purchases that Ervin had made. I walked back over to him and emptied the envelope at his feet.

"I'm goin' to make this easy for you. We can sell this house, I get the money from that, and I want eight million, and you can just move around the corner with your family," I said as I made my way over to the bar in our living room to get some more wine.

"Look, we can work this out," Ervin pleaded as he picked up the contents from the envelope.

"There isn't anything to work out. You were not only sleeping with my sister, you got her pregnant. I don't know how long y'all little thing was goin' on, but I do know that you have a five-year-old daughter named Brittney Marie Simmons. So that means you've probably been fuckin' with Samantha for six years. You better be lucky that all my test results came back negative."

"If this is how you want it to be, Milan, then we'll just let the judge decide."

"That's cool. I'll get half of everything. Thanks for loving me so much that you cleared our shared bank accounts. Oh, I forgot you left five hundred dollars."

Ervin sat down on the couch and leaned back, staring up at the ceiling as I sat down on the loveseat. He hadn't said anything, but I knew that he was thinking. Knowing that this would get nasty, and considering the average deal he got his clients were forty million and up, eight million was nothing to him. Ervin had other business ventures, and money hadn't been an issue for him in a long time. Perfect opportunities just seemed to always fall in his lap.

"I'll get you the eight million in a few days," Ervin said after five minutes.

I reached over to get my phone off the end table and called his accountant and handed him the phone. He wasn't talking to somebody that he could bullshit, and I knew that he could get that done right now. He was not about to string me along for another moment.

"You want the money, you need to pack everything that you can in eight minutes and leave and never come back," Ervin suggested, ending the call as his accountant repeatedly said hello.

"Get the fuck out of my house!" I screamed, and he didn't budge.

I pulled out my nine that was still in my purse from me going to the shooting range when I left from viewing the home earlier. I got up from the couch, and his eyes bulged out of his head in disbelief that I would pull a gun he purchased out on him.

"So, you must have been fuckin' that thug ass nigga for a while if you think that you can pull a gun out on me," he finally said, standing up with his hands in the air as I walked up on him.

"Technically, this is my house, and I have the paperwork to prove that. It's not my fault your crack head momma fucked up your credit so bad that you couldn't go on the loan with me?"

"My momma doesn't have anything to do with what's goin' on with us."

"She raised your sorry ass," I said, ushering him to the door as he walked backwards.

"We will just let the judge decide everything else from here on out. Don't call me, don't text me, and most importantly, don't ever come here again!" I said, letting off a shot into the ceiling, and he ran out of the front door I had opened for him.

My work phone started vibrating in my purse, and it was a text from Amayah asking me could she go with her uncle Chris to a Nuggets game tomorrow. I let her know that she could while I waited for the police to come because I knew one of nosy ass neighbors had already called.

Chapter Seven

CHRISTOPHER "GUNNA" ROGERS"

"What the fuck do you mean it's short?" I spat as I paced the floor.

"Man, it's not right. I did exactly what Nightmare told me to do, and all the money ain't there. I talked to all them niggas that dropped off money, and they all sayin' it ain't them," Butta replied.

"Why the fuck are you letting these niggas leave without verifying the money isn't right?"

"That nigga Roc said that I was moving too slow and—" Butta attempted to say but was cut off.

"The only muthafuckas that tell you what to do when it comes to this shit here is me or Nightmare!"

I made my way out of the back of the club, leaving Butta with his thoughts. He should have known better, but I knew with the way that nigga Roc threw his position around that he felt that he needed to listen to him. But that shit was dead. I made my way up to the VIP where I knew that nigga Roc was at.

"I need to holla at you!" I yelled over the music as I moved the rope and walked in his section.

All these bitches and random ass niggas were lookin' at me, but I didn't know none of these muthafuckas except his little brother, so they knew damn well I wasn't talking to them. Roc heard me, and these niggas and bitches that were drinkin' on his dime all were still partyin' because he hadn't given the word to get the fuck on. I went and stood by the balcony and whistled, catchin' the DJ's attention. I signaled for him to cut the music; it abruptly stopped, making the crowd scream.

"I don't know if you think I'm playin' or what, but everybody that isn't Big Roc needs to clear out this fuckin' section!" I spat, sittin' down on the couch across from Roc and pullin' my tool out the back of my jeans, placing it on my lap.

The muthafuckas downstairs and on the dancefloor were goin' crazy, ready to start a fuckin' riot. All the niggas except Baby Roc were trippin' over the bitches to get out of the section. Baby Roc knew who was runnin' shit, so he knew it was best if he got the fuck on. He was as close to his brother as I was to mine, so whatever this nigga had been allowing, he knew about it. Once the section was cleared, I sent the DJ a text to start the music.

"What the fuck make you think that you got the authority to tell niggas how to handle the money? Nigga, yo' job is to distribute the shit, nothin' else. What the fuck is you doin', takin' the money buyin' that jewelry you got on? You took that bitch from dressing out of Walmart to Fashion Nova, I see that. You got her hair and nails done, but the bitch still ain't yours. Let me show you."

"Ayye, baby in the white dress, come here!" I yelled out, and she looked around tryin' to make sure I was talkin' to her as I waved her over.

Lookin' at this nigga Roc, he was hurt and pissed the fuck off, but not as hurt as he was goin' to be when I was finished with his ass. The bitch hurried back over to the section, smiling from ear to ear. Roc's glare went from me to her as she made her way over to me with her back turned to him.

"Go downstairs and meet me in the front," I said, and she bit on her lip and made her way out the booth and downstairs.

"So, I'm gon' fuck yo' bitch and pass her back to the hood. Nigga and you goin' back to the trap. Clearly you can't handle yo' position, so I'm gon' take that off yo' hands."

"What the fuck did Nightmare say 'bout this?" Roc questioned.

"Nigga, don't question my muthafuckin authority," I spat, jumpin' up with my tool in my hand.

I wasn't worried about the cameras; I owned this bitch, and whenever I walked in, all the cameras went fuzzy. As far as any of these muthafuckas in here, these niggas bled just like me, and if they wanted to take it there, we could. But it wasn't a secret how the fuck I got down. Everybody in this bitch knew who I was, and my name spoke for itself.

"Look, Gunna—" Roc pleaded.

"Nigga, I don't need to look at shit. You heard what the fuck I said, and I ain't never been one for repeating myself. Unless you want to handle this shit another way, then we can do that too. So just let me fuckin' know how you want to do this shit."

A few minutes passed, and this nigga was weighing his options. I had a little patience, but not much when it came to bullshit.

"Tick tock, muthafucka. So, what's it gon' be?"

"I'll play this shit yo' way," Roc said, but his eyes told me a different story.

"I thought you would see things my way. I'll be in touch," I said, slippin' my tool in the back of my jeans as I stood up.

"Don't worry. She gon' suck my dick; she not pretty enough to be blessed with anything else. Enjoy yo' night," I said in between laughin'.

He might have had the money, or he might have just been lettin' niggas pay some and give the rest on the back end, but either way, that shit wasn't authorized, and he knew better. Roc was Nightmare's people, not mine. Because he had been so solid and held shit down, Nightmare thought he would be perfect for the position. I knew he wasn't, and I let Nightmare know, but he still gave it to him.

As I made my way downstairs, the crowd split, making a path for me to get through. Bitches that I wouldn't touch were damn near foaming at the mouth, and niggas that wished they could even have a conversation with me were either looking on in admiration or hate. As long as they stayed in their place, they could look as much as they wanted.

Lookin' ahead, this girl was standin' at the end of my path. Pretty chocolate skin, long black hair that was all hers, thick thighs, and pretty brown eyes. She had her arms folded across her chest and was muggin' the fuck out of me. I remember when I used to love her ass, the only girl that I had ever loved outside of my family. You couldn't tell me shit about her because she was mine, and no matter what, she was gon' always be. I didn't fuck things up; she did, and she had to live with the consequences.

"Christopher, we need to talk," Maddison said once I made it up to where she was standing.

"We don't have shit to talk about. Move, Maddie," I said as she held her stance.

"Please, can we talk? Just for a minute, please." Maddison begged with tears forming in her eyes.

"Move, Maddison, damn," I said as a security guard that I hadn't ever seen walked up on us like he was ready to move her.

"Nigga, don't fuckin' touch her," I spat, and Maddie jumped by the sound of my voice.

The new nigga hurried away as I walked around Maddison, and she screamed my government name as I made my way out the door. I made my way to my car that was parked out front.

My nigga Tech was standing by my truck. He handled the business shit with the club for me.

"That new nigga that you got doing that security shit, you need to let him know who the fuck he better not ever fuckin' lay a hand on," I said as we shook up.

Tech nodded his head, and I jumped into my truck. It was about to be a long night. I knew that Nightmare was goin' to want shit handled another way, but he put me in charge, so I was doin' shit how I saw fit. My phone started ringing, and it was Tech. I already knew that he was calling about Maddie, and I had some important shit to worry 'bout right now.

I knew that Nightmare was goin' to have some shit to say 'bout the way that I was handling things, but I was doin' what was best for everybody. My brother shot first, and the situation with Ike was the first time I had ever heard him ask any questions. I knew that he was tryin' to step back to handle shit with my niece. Even though he hadn't said anything to me about it yet, I knew that he was gettin' tired of this shit.

Right now, we only had a few niggas left, and we couldn't take another loss right now. I knew that Roc wasn't goin' to just take his new position quietly, but in the meantime, I had more important shit to worry about. Nightmare didn't seem to be worried about the shit with the feds, but shit, I was. Right now, we needed to have as many niggas in the streets as possible, and I'd keep spinning Roc in the direction I wanted him to go.

As I made my way to have a sit down with the rest of our team, my phone rang. It was a call I'd been waiting on, so I answered, and her voice boomed through the speakers in my truck.

"Thank you, Uncle Gunna, for getting me out the house and the clothes too," Amayah said as we got into the truck.

"You know that Uncle got you. You weren't gon' be goin' nowhere with me lookin' like a bum," I assured her.

"I'm tryin' not to complain because my dad at least gave me my phone back, but I miss my car."

Shit, I couldn't believe that she got that bitch back, but he still had her eating like an inmate, and all that was in her room was the mattress and box spring. I turned up Meek Mill as we made our way to Nana's so I could drop off this shit for this baby. I knew that I was goin' to have to hear her mouth because she still had the baby, but shit, we couldn't find this bitch Gia.

"Uncle Gunna, you need to tell my dad that he should get with Milan," Amayah said.

"What's up with you and that lady? Why you think she should fuck with yo' dad? I don't know if that's a good idea," I admitted.

"Uncle Gunna, he's getting old, and he needs somebody so he can stay out of my business so much."

Amayah and I talked because she decided to turn the music down for the rest of our twenty-minute drive.

"I don't want to go in. Nana doesn't like me," Amayah whined as I pulled in Nana's driveway.

"Well, she really gon' talk about you when you don't come in," I said as I gathered up the baby shit and made my way in the house through the back door.

"What is Bonnie doin' sittin' in the damn car? She steals anything out of here, and I'll break her fuckin' hand!" Nana spat as I walked into the kitchen.

"Hi, Nana. How are you doing?" I asked and sat down at the island in the kitchen, and she wasted no time handing me the baby as soon as I sat all the stuff down.

"So, who's the bitch that dropped off the baby over here again?" Nana asked as I played with Kiara.

"Kiara, Nana. I'm goin' to get her soon. I just have to finish getting the house together," I replied as Amayah came in the back door.

"I wondered how long ya black ass was goin' to sit in that damn car. You always been weird just like ya damn momma!" Nana yelled.

"Nana, I was on the phone with my dad," Amayah pleaded, attempting to hug and kiss her.

"You a lyin' ass bitch too. I know whoever the nigga is, you gotta be fuckin' and suckin' him. Don't kiss me, hell!"

"Nana, you trippin'. Chill," I threw in, but I could tell by the look on Amayah's face that it was some truth in what Nana was sayin', and that shit broke my heart.

Amayah was like my baby and always had been since

Nightmare brought her to the house after she was born. She told me that she was dealing with a nigga, but she wouldn't tell me his name. She told me about the car situation, but I knew she was leaving shit out. I knew how I dealt with my sister's baby dad, so it was best if I don't know the truth for now.

"Back to this damn baby. Christopher, I done raised all of my kids. You gotta get this damn baby. I already got your sister and these damn demon seeds in here. It's too many damn people for one house!" Nana insisted.

"Uncle Gunna, whose baby is this?" Amayah asked.

"Amayah!" one of the twins yelled, and Nana ushered her out the kitchen.

"Nana, I just need a little more time. I'm goin' to be takin' her home soon," I assured her.

"When the fuck is soon? Come on over here to this calendar and show me that damn date on here!"

As I played with Kiara, she smiled back at me. She made me think about my life and the shit that I wanted. I wanted a family, but none of the bitches that I fucked with were the one that I would want to carry my child. I fucked with a few bitches here and there, but I was not gon' be the nigga with a bunch of baby mommas.

Lookin' around the kitchen, I really wished Nana would let us upgrade her house. I offered for her to come to my house, and she wouldn't. Shit, that was after Nightmare brought her a brand-new house that she wouldn't even go and see. I don't know why she wouldn't leave this damn house, but I wished she would. As much as she complained

about it every damn day, she would not leave the fuckin'
hood.

I sat and talked to Nana for about twenty minutes, and
after a while, Nana took the baby from me. But she claimed
she was so ready for her to go. The scent of the food she was
cooking had my stomach growling. As soon as Nana took her,
I made my way out the back door and texted Amayah and
told her to get out here ASAP, and as she came runnin' out
the house, I could hear Nana screaming. As soon as Amayah
got in the truck, I got a text from this bitch Mo, and I
ignored it and made my way to the game.

We made our way to the stadium after about ten minutes.
I handed my keys to the valet as he opened my door.

"Girl, I ain't yo' daddy. Get the hell out!" I said and
Amayah rolled her eyes but got out.

"Keep my shit up here!" I advised the valet, and we made
our way into the arena.

We made our way up to my skybox, and Amayah was doin'
somethin' on her phone like always. As we walked into the sky
box, I peeped Maddison sitting across the room. When we
made eye contact, she mugged the fuck out of a nigga, but
that was nothin' new. My bitch Nikki and her sister Simone
were on the other side of the room. Nikki's face lit up when
she saw a nigga, so I made my way over to her.

"TT Maddie with the fattie!" Amayah screamed, runnin'
toward Maddie.

"Hey, baby," Nikki sang as she jumped up to hug me.

"How was your day?" I asked Nikki.

"Hump," Simone said, cuttin' Nikki off.

Nikki put her sister in her place, and I gave her my attention after she assured me that she was good. The bitch Simone didn't like me and hadn't ever, so I didn't know why the fuck she was even here. I made my way over to my cousins Skitzo and Sierra as my bitch Kelsey came in the sky box.

"Nigga, you always fuckin' late," Skitzo said as I sat down.

"You need to fuckin' go talk to Maddison," Sierra threw in.

"You go fuckin' talk to her. I ain't the bitch's therapist," I spat.

"You ain't shit!" Sierra screamed and got up and made her way over to Maddison.

"You put yo'self in this situation. Still allowing her ass to come around. You know how Sierra and Honey are when it comes to her. You need to cut her ass off, all the fuckin' way. Nigga, you done did all that you can do. I get it; you got a fuckin' conscience. Nigga, in this shit, you can't have one," Skitzo said as Amayah made her way over to where we were.

"Hey, Sicari," Amayah said as she hugged Skitzo and sat down next to me.

I sat watching the game for about twenty minutes, and Amayah was smackin' her gum in my ear.

"Uncle G, why would you have all these girls here, knowing that Maddie was going to be here?" Amayah asked as Kelsey brought over our food.

"Uncle G!" Daisy and Blossom screamed as they came runnin' across the room to where we were sitting.

I hugged Daisy and Blossom like I hadn't just seen them a

little while ago, and they made their way over to their seats. Amayah was waiting for an answer, and I got it; she fucked with Maddie, but she didn't know our situation. The only person that did was Skitzo, and that was why he said the shit that he did.

"Amayah, stay out of my business 'cause yo' ass don't have to eat. I ain't holdin' nobody hostage, and I didn't invite nobody here but Nikki. They can all chill and watch the game, or they can all get the fuck on!" I said loud enough for everybody to hear.

"Why would you have all these girls here knowing that Maddie comes here every home game?" Honey questioned as she walked up behind me.

"Honey, stay out my fuckin' business, damn!" I yelled, not taking my eyes off the game.

"Twins, put on y'all headphones!" I ordered, and they put them on fast because they knew that I was about to say some shit that they didn't need to hear.

"Does anybody have a fuckin' problem? Because the way I see it, I paid for all the weave, nails, and clothes that everybody—" I said before Sierra jumped up.

"First of muthafuckin of all, you didn't pay for none of my shit!" Sierra screamed.

"Well, if it don't apply, let it fly! But everybody else, y'all know what it is," I said, and Sierra sat her ass back down.

"Nigga, you didn't pay for my shit either," Skitzo threw in.

"Everybody that shares the same blood as me, shut the hell up!"

"But the rest of y'all know what it is. And before you fix yo' coke head mouth, Simone, I know that all the shit you got on is Nikki's, including them old ass tracks, so you don't say shit either, because I ain't talkin' to you.

"Like the fuck I was sayin', if you don't want to be here, then there is the door. I ain't put no voodoo spell on none of y'all asses, so when you see fit, you can be on yo' way. Just make sure you ready for whatever comes next. Don't nobody need to say shit else to me until the game is over!"

I sat back down in my seat, and Amayah was just lookin' at me, shaking her head. I knew that her and most of my family were close with Maddison, but at the end of the day, me and her would never be together again. As I ate and glanced up at the halftime show here and there, I got a text message from Roc. I didn't even waste my time reading that shit. I knew by now word had got back to him about how shit was goin' down. When I was ready to talk to his ass we'd sit down, and not a second before.

Lookin' over my shoulder because my sister and cousin couldn't whisper and I could hear all the shit they are talkin' like I wasn't in the same fuckin' room. After I said what needed to be said, they went right into talkin' their shit. When my eyes landed on Maddison, she had the same look she always had whenever she saw a nigga. Everybody else was smilin' and wasn't shit wrong with them. I knew what was wrong, but it wasn't shit that I could do for her. She needed to just let the shit go.

They all knew about each other; it wasn't a secret. They all assumed that Maddison held some position that she didn't. Our situation was complicated. Hell, she didn't even have my phone number.

I turned back around because I didn't give a fuck what nobody had to say 'bout how I handled my shit. At the end of the day, this was what the fuck it was goin' to be. I felt somebody tap me on my shoulder, so I turned, and it was Daisy. I took her headphones off because she was askin' could they take them off now. She made her way back over to Blossom, and she took hers off too.

This used to be somethin' that me and Ike did with our families. He brought his girl and their kids, and I brought my family to all the home games. I hadn't been the same since my nigga had been gone, but it wasn't shit that I could do about it. When Nightmare had his mind made up, it wasn't shit that anybody could do to change it.

After about twenty minutes, once the game started back up, I gave my attention to the game as Skitzo talked his shit, mad because he was 'bout to have to give up twenty stacks because the Nuggets were winning.

"Nigga. These muthafuckas ain't playin'. I got ten on me. I'm gon' have to run to the house and get the other ten," Skitzo spat.

"Then nigga you need to leave now to go and get my muthafuckin money," I said in between laughin, because I knew his ass was lying.

"Who are you texting?" I asked Amayah.

"My friend," she replied, not even lookin' up from her phone.

"Why can't I know this nigga's name?" I asked.

She hadn't said anything or even looked up from her phone. She was typing so damn fast. She must've been sending damn paragraphs to whoever this nigga was.

"Uncle Gunna, would you ever hit any of your girls?" Amayah asked after 'bout ten minutes.

"Everybody get the fuck out!" I said, and everybody froze up and stopped all their conversations.

"None of y'all don't have a hearing aid, so I know that y'all can hear. Get the fuck out!"

Everybody jumped up but Skitzo and Amayah and were damn near fallin' over each other tryin' to get out the room.

"Why the hell you askin' me that? Somebody done fuckin' hit you?" I asked.

"Don't lie. If you lie, it's just goin' to make it worse," Skitzo threw in, too damn calm for me.

"No, I'm just askin' would you. Uncle Gunna, calm down and relax. I'm good," Amayah said, rolling her eyes as I paced the floor.

"Naw, I don't hit females, but I want to know why the hell would you ask me somethin' like that. Is somethin' goin' on that I need to know about, Amayah? Because if I find out you're lyin', we're goin' to have a problem," I advised her.

"What the fuck you tryin' to say? I look like I'd hit a bitch?" I asked after silence filled the room for too long for me.

"Yeah, you do, and look how you talk to them. My dad won't even talk to females around me, so I just wondered. One of my friends said that her boyfriend was hittin' her, but she was tryin' to say that he loved her and this and that, so I just wondered. That's all, Uncle. Sit down. It's not that serious."

"Amayah, is some nigga puttin' his fuckin' hands on you?" I asked once I got back in front of her.

"No, Uncle Gunna. I promise," Amayah said, lookin' me dead in the eyes.

"Everybody that shares my last name, come back in. The rest of y'all, time's up. Good night!" I yelled as I sat back down, lookin' at Amayah.

"Uncle, I'm good. You know that if somethin' was wrong I'd come to you. I tell you everything," Amayah pleaded. As I turned around, Maddison was walkin' her ass back in the room with the rest of my family.

"Well, her last name is Rogers," Honey said, throwing her hands up in the air like Maddison needed an interpreter.

"Honey, don't get cussed out tryin' to take anotha muthafucka's side. You remember at the end of the day, you're my muthafuckin sister!" I spat

"Right is right, and wrong is wrong," Honey replied.

"That's why them bitches be thinking she yo' wife. How the fuck you kick all them out, and she gets to stay? Nigga, you gon' be stuck with her ass forever," Skitzo said, shaking his head.

I knew that I had to get a handle on this shit with Maddison. It had been goin' on for years now. It only kept getting worse, and I knew that Skitzo was right. I had to cut all ties from her. Everybody assumed that I still have feelings for her, but that wasn't the case. I still kept her close and took care of her because I was responsible for the death of her parents. She didn't know that, and I couldn't look her in the eyes and tell her that.

I was young, and I was moving too fast, and I didn't give a fuck how my actions affected anybody else. I never thought that shit would come back to them, but it did. Maddison didn't have any brothers or sisters, and the family that she did have left when they found out about me, they cut ties. Even though we'd been done for years, she hadn't even attempted to get back right with them.

Maddison stood ten toes down with me when it came to her family and friends, but in the streets, she had me out here looking like a goofy. Here I was thinking that my bitch was loyal and had my back. Come to find out, she was fuckin' with some broke ass nigga. She was always complaining that I was never around and was always in the streets. I wasn't fuckin' bitches or on no bullshit. I was gettin' money, but because I didn't make it home at six o'clock every night for dinner, we always had an issue. Instead of talkin' to me about the shit, she let Roc get in her head and the pussy that I thought was mine.

Chapter Eight

NIGHTMARE

"Where the money at? All this other shit is irrelevant. I don't give a fuck about yo' crack-head momma or none of that shit you talkin' 'bout," I spat at Boo.

We were sittin' at a table in the middle of a warehouse that I used when discussin' business with my workers. After talkin' to Iman, I had to be sure to cover all my bases. I couldn't be seen talkin' to any known criminals, so even though I wanted to go to where this nigga laid his head at before he got out of bed, I couldn't.

"Nightmare, I just need a couple of days to come up with the rest of it. I got half," Boo pleaded as I looked over at Gunna.

I asked Gunna to hold shit down while I got Amayah back on track, and clearly, I was askin' for too much because this nigga was lettin' niggas get shit on consignment. If you didn't have the money, you couldn't get shit from me, and Boo knew that. More importantly, Gunna knew that.

"You got half? Well how many days you think you need to get the rest?" I asked.

"Four to five days max. I got my people workin' nonstop. Shit, it might be even sooner," Boo assured, moving his hands like a bitch.

Pulling out my blade and reachin' across the table, I grabbed Boo's hand, and one by one, cut off all his fingers on his left hand, leaving his thumb.

"Urrrgh! Ni-Night... Man, I swear on my grandma's grave I'm goin' to get your money!" Boo cried out in pain.

"In four of five days?" I asked, still holdin' his hand and pressin' it into the table.

"Mannn. Look—"

"You got five hours," I spat and swiftly cut off his thumb.

"Throw that nigga's finger and thumb into the fireplace," I ordered and got up, makin' my way out the building.

My nigga Mone moved swiftly and gathered up his fingers and completed the task. I made my way to my car, and Gunna took his time making his way out as I sat in my car waitin' for this nigga.

"Gunna, if you want out, say that shit now, but quit actin' like Ike was yo' bitch! That nigga gone, and he ain't fuckin' coming back! This shit is unacceptable!" I roared as soon as Gunna was in the car and the door was closed.

"Nigga, fuck you! I didn't give the green light for him to

get that shit. Yo' nigga Roc, that you trust and put in charge of distribution, did that bullshit. Nigga, I'm not out here moving flawed. I'm not in my feelings like a bitch over Ike!"

"I handled the shit with Roc already," Gunna advised me as I started up the car and pulled away from the warehouse.

"This type of shit can't be happening. We need to have a certain amount of money on hand that if shit falls down, we can touch. That is why shit is set up the way that it is," I said, tryin' to calm down because he wasn't the one that fucked up.

"Nigga, I know. That is why I'm handling distribution. That nigga Roc got demoted. I know you said that we are good right now, but I can't take no chances."

"Demoted and what else?"

"Fucked his wife and took his kids out for ice cream today," Gunna said in between laughin'.

"That's not what the fuck I had in mind. Niggas start moving off emotions when bitches get involved. Did you think about that?"

"Fuck that nigga," Gunna spat.

I didn't know what the fuck Gunna's issue was with Roc, but he had always had one. He never spoke on it, and I didn't have time to play guessin' games. At this point, it didn't matter. Gunna was a grown ass man, and he shouldn't have stepped to that nigga's wife, but if she gave a fuck about her wedding vows, she wouldn't have fucked with him. Involving the nigga's kids was what had my mind runnin', because if yo' bitch gon' fuck, she gon' fuck. But if a nigga was anywhere around my kids, him and the bitch would be dead.

I made my way to Nana's to take Gunna to his truck. As I pulled into the driveway, Faith was coming out of the house.

"Nigga, why don't you fuck with Faith? She here already. You clearly need some more pussy since you always got so much to say about my bitches," Gunna suggested.

"Ayye, Faith, come here real quick!" Gunna called out as we got out the car.

"Nigga, where you goin'? I'm tryin' to hook you up!" Gunna yelled out as I made my way in the house.

I'd never fuck with Faith like that, and Gunna already knew that. Faith was beautiful and smart, but she was family. It was some shit that you just don't do. Faith was Amayah's god mom. I trusted her with my daughter and my home, and it wasn't too many people that I gave that type of trust to.

"That's who you need to be with, Fay- Fay! Instead of fuckin' that girl that you won't even see when the sun is up!" Nana said as I made my way through her house.

I made my way to take out the trash. Even though I sent Faith over here to go to the store and make sure she was good, I knew that Nana didn't let her take out the trash because she thought that I was the designated garbage man. Gunna needed to be taking out the trash. That nigga was always over here eating, if he wasn't at my house.

"Maurice!"

"Maur-muthafuckin-rice!" Nana screamed as I came back in the back door.

I ignored her and flipped through the mail on her table. After a few minutes of me getting sick of hearing her scream,

I made my way to the living room where she was sittin'. I sat down on the couch across from her, but now, she all of a sudden didn't have anything to say. Why couldn't I have a nice grandma that baked cookies and loved to see her grandkids?

"What's up, Nana?"

"Don't ever in yo' muthafuckin life make me call yo' black ass that many times and you not come see what the fuck I want fast!" Nana yelled, turnin' down the news that is blarin'.

"Yo' sister has lost her muthafuckin mind. You need to talk to her dumb ass. I'm sick of lookin' at her and the damn flowers. I live alone for a reason. When I wanted the hoe to come live with me, she didn't want to. Now the bitch is here every night. What type of mother just takes they damn kids from pillar to post every damn day?"

"Huh, muthafucka? You raised the bitch," Nana asked.

"Nana, Honey is grown. You know how I feel about her fuckin' up. You know all the shit that I did so she could—"

"Here the dummy come now. Roses and Petals, take off them damn shoes!" Nana screamed cuttin' me off.

Honey didn't even look in my direction. She ushered the kids upstairs after they all took their shoes off. I busted my ass to make sure that Honey was afforded all of the opportunities that I never had. She was on the right track until she met her babies' dad, Mack. Honey didn't come to me with her shit until it was to the point that she couldn't fix it.

She called Gunna, and he dished out money to her. She knew that if she told Gunna what was really goin' on, her baby daddy would be on a t-shirt. I saw Honey or talked to her every day, and I knew that somethin' is goin' on with her, but I kept waiting for her to say somethin'.

"Why isn't she at her house?" I asked.

"Ask her!" Nana screamed.

"I'll talk to her, Nana. I gotta go and handle some business. Do you need anything before I go?"

"When are you goin' to settle down and have a family? You know who I want you to be with. Hell, what are you waiting for?"

"Bye, Nana," I said as I got up to leave.

"Bye, Nana my ass. You need to take yo' sister and them kids with you!"

"We need to talk," I said as Honey did the cheer moves like she was on the basketball court with them.

She acted like she didn't hear me, so I hit her arm, and she turned and gave me a dirty ass look. When I called her, she didn't answer, and I knew that fuckin' phone stayed glued to her at all times. I showed up at her fuckin' house a few times, and her ass was not ever there. When Nana called me last night sayin' that she had a dream about somethin' bad happening to Honey, I promised her that I would talk to her, but I hadn't had the time.

Nana swore she was a fuckin' physic, but when I called her that, she went the fuck off and went into this shit about her being a prophet. Even though I knew that Nana was fuckin' crazy as hell, she meant well. I was sure Honey had told Nana what she wanted her to know about what she was goin' through, but Nana would never tell me.

"What the fuck is y'all baldhead ass lookin' at?" I asked, getting sick of Daisy and Blossom staring down my damn tonsils.

"We got hair!" Blossom yelled.

"That ain't hair, baby, but don't worry. Uncle Gunna can buy y'all some," I said.

"Why are you always fuckin' with my kids?" Honey spat, tryin' to hit me, but I blocked it.

"I didn't do shit to them. They always fuckin' with me. Especially the fuckin' blind one with them thick ass glasses. I didn't know they made them for kids," I said, and Blossom jumped up like she was ready to fight.

"Honey, get yo' bad ass kids under control," I said, handing them some money to get some snacks and get the fuck out of my face for a minute.

Scanning the gym, I spotted Gunna all in some bitch's face. I knew he didn't bring one of them dumb ass bitches to my baby's cheerleading competition. Every bitch he met, he wanted to bring around and make her feel special. He knew better than to bring any of them ratchet bitches to my house, but clearly, he thought that bringing her here would win her over. I shook my head as he got closer, and I realized that the bitch Gunna was with was Milan.

"Baby, this is a once in a lifetime opportunity. You'll never meet another nigga like me!" Gunna said as Milan turned her back on him and made her way over to two niggas.

"Nigga, do you just try to talk to every bitch you see?" I asked as he came over to where Honey, Faith, and I were sitting on the bleachers.

"Nigga, don't be mad because bitches want me!" Gunna yelled over the people cheering.

"Stay away from that one," I warned.

"Why?" Honey said, turnin' around.

"None of yo' fuckin' business. Worry about where that nigga is at in yo' truck," I said, and she turned around fast.

I turned, and Milan was staring at me, half smiling until I stuck up my middle finger at her ass. She rolled her eyes and focused her attention on doin' somethin' on her phone. She was supposed to be here for Amayah, but here she was in some niggas' faces. Amayah's team was done for the first round, and the other girls huddled with the coach, and Amayah started joggin' toward us.

"What the fuck did one of these bitches do to my baby?" I asked as I ran down the bleachers to meet her.

"Dad, nothin'. Why you always gotta act so crazy?" Amayah asked, rolling her eyes and folding her arms across her chest.

"What the fuck is wrong?" I asked, because somethin' wasn't right.

"I don't feel good. My head has been hurting' all morning. That medicine isn't working'," Amayah whined, clinging' onto my arm.

"Well come on. We can go home," I said, waving' Honey, and 'em down.

"Naw, I want to stay and see them finish, Dad." Amayah whined as Milan walked over to us.

"Hey, Amayah, how are you doin'?" Milan asked, rubbin' Amayah's free arm.

"You made it. Thank you so much for coming," Amayah said, letting go of me and huggin' Milan.

"What's wrong?" Milan asked, pretending to be concerned.

"She didn't come to see you. Don't let her ass lie to you. She came to see some nigga, baby," I said, making Milan turn her head to look at me.

"Dad, shut up, dang," Amayah said, tryin' to stick up for this bitch, like I wasn't the nigga that I am.

"Who is that?'" Honey asked as Amayah and Milan walked away with that bitch holdin' my baby, like she was hers.

"Her case manager. I keep tellin' Amayah that she the fuckin' police whether she got a badge and gun or not," I said.

"Shut up. She is not the police. From what Amayah told me, she's cool, and she likes her. You know that she's not a mean asshole like you. She sees the good in people and gives people a chance, unlike you," Honey said, elbowing me.

"Who the fuck is that bitch, and why is she over there consoling my daughter?" I heard a familiar voice say from behind me, making me turn around.

"Bitch, what the fuck are you even doin' here? Yo' bitch ass had my baby sittin' in front of yo' momma's for over two hours, and yo' punk ass couldn't even answer the phone and tell her that you weren't coming. Get the fuck away from me before I break yo' fuckin' neck. Do not go over there and say a fuckin' word to my daughter," I spat with Honey clingin' onto my arm and Gunna tryin' to tell me to calm down.

"Fuck you, Nightmare! That's my fuckin' daughter too. You can't keep me away from her."

"Bitch, you want to try and see?" I asked in between looking back as I saw Amayah and Milan walk out of the gym.

"Nadia, just fuckin' go," Honey begged her.

When Nadia and I locked eyes again, she contemplated her next move for a few seconds and then made her way out of the gym, goin' in the opposite direction of where Amayah went.

"Maybe we should go. Is Amayah still not feelin' good?" Honey suggested.

"I'm not goin' nowhere," I spat.

"Bitch, you need to mind yo' fuckin' business and worry about yo' daughter that's fuckin' everybody on the basketball team. That is why that bitch over there scratchin' herself. You need to take that hoe to the clinic!" I yelled as I looked over, and this white bitch was all in my fuckin' business.

I made my way back to my seat with Gunna by my side and Honey behind us. I didn't know what the fuck would make that bitch think that today and here would be the place for her to see Amayah. Amayah had been dealin' with enough. I was not about to let that bitch fuck up today. The intermission was almost over, and I still didn't see Amayah or Milan.

"Where are you goin'?" Honey asked as I got up to go and find them.

"To find my baby."

"Nigga, she is not a fuckin' baby," Gunna said in between laughin'.

I didn't respond. For Nadia's sake, she better be the fuck out of here, and Amayah better not have seen her. Amayah called Nadia's triflin' ass for a week straight, and she never answered her calls. She even tried to text the bitch off of my phone and got no response. When I tried to talk to her about it, she didn't want to talk. I knew that it was eventually goin' to be a conversation that we were goin' to have to have. I had always wanted her to form her own opinion, but I was not goin' to keep letting that bitch play with my baby's feelings either.

As I looked around outside of the gym, I didn't see Amayah or Milan, so I pulled out my phone to call Milan. Before I could press call, I saw them coming out of the bathroom. I knew that Amayah forming this bond with Milan had a lot to do with her not having many women around her other than the women in our family. I damn sure didn't want her to be nothin' like Honey.

"Why don't you go and have yo' own baby? Why are you doin' all of this?" I asked as they walked over to where I was standing.

"Maurice, I know there is a theory that people in the system don't give a fuck about you, and you were just a number to them. I'm not them. I actually do care about my clients. I'm not doin' anything for Amayah that I wouldn't do for any of my other clients," Milan insisted.

"My head is starting to feel better," Amayah said and downed a bottle of water.

"What did you give my daughter? Some fuckin' drugs that you stole from the evidence room?" I asked.

"Where I work, we don't have an evidence room. I gave her some pain medicine. Do you want to see the bottle?" Milan asked while digging in her purse.

"Dad, I'm goin' to go and finish the competition. Please don't run Milan away," Amayah said and ran back into the gym.

"Girl, I want to see that damn medicine bottle," I said as she tried to hand me a medicine bottle.

"Maurice, you told me to make sure I was here. I can leave," Milan suggested, waiting for a response.

"You came here for them niggas you were sittin' with. You not about to make me the bad guy and have Amayah not talkin' to me. If she drop a hot UA for them funny pills in that big ass purse, you gon' be explaining that shit to your supervisor," I said, and I made my way back in the gym with Milan not far behind.

I made it back over to Honey and Gunna, and as I sat down, I saw Milan was behind me coming up to where we were sitting. As she went to sit down in front of me, I blocked her with my foot.

"You can take yo' ass back over there to them niggas that

you were sitting with. We don't do the police in this section," I spat with my eyes on Amayah.

"For the last and final time, I'm not the fuckin' police," Milan said, tryin' to whisper, sitting down next to me.

"Milan!" A young nigga called out from the bottom of the bleachers.

"Go on to yo' nigga. I'll tell Amayah that you had to go," I said, shooing her ass away.

Milan waved at the nigga and gave her attention back to me.

"Maurice, I can tell that you're used to females backing down from you and being scared of you, but I'm not," Milan tried to read me.

A few seconds had passed, and Milan was still just staring at a nigga.

"Boo!" I spat, turnin' to look at her ass, and she jumped, terrified.

"I can't tell you ain't scared," I said, shaking my head.

"Huh, give these to my niece. I gotta go pick up that girl," Gunna said, handing me flowers, and made his way down the bleachers.

I nodded my head because I knew that Skitzo had finally got Gia. I was letting Gunna step up, so now this was his time to shine and to handle shit. It was hard for me to let anybody lead the ship that I had been leading for so long, but I knew that I have to put more time into my daughter right now. I couldn't let her get lost out here, because once a good girl was gone, she was gone forever. I refused to let my baby be like any of these rat ass bitches out here if I had anything to do with it.

"Why you been over here so much?" I asked Honey as I poured myself a drink in Nana's kitchen.

"I hope you washed yo' damn hands before you got in my damn refrigerator drinkin' my damn juice!" Nana yelled from the other room.

"Nana, chill. I washed my hands, damn."

"When, nigga, yesterday? Because them fingernails is dirty as hell like you been playing in the dirt. I hope yo' nasty ass ain't been touchin' nobody with them nasty ass hands!" Nana threw in.

Ignoring Nana, I gave my attention back to Honey. Honey put her phone down and took a deep breath, thinking about what to say to me. I heard what sounded like a baby whining. It must've been one of the twins' toys, but that shit sounded real as hell.

"Say, what the fuck is on yo' mind. I didn't raise you to bite yo' tongue for nobody," I spat.

"Nightmare, I know how you feel about Mack. You've never made it a secret, and I never come to you unless shit is all fucked up, and I've been tryin' to handle this on my own. I can't keep running to my brothers every time something is wrong."

"Cut the shit. Where the fuck is yo' truck, and why are y'all stayin' over here?"

"Tell his ass, so he can handle the shit before I do!" Nana yelled, still in the other room.

"How the hell can you hear anything over that loud ass TV?" I asked, because I really want to know.

"Because God gave me two ears, so I can hear, muthafucka!" Nana replied.

At seventy years old, you would think somebody grandma would be sleep at this time of night, but clearly not her ass. I didn't know when the fuck she slept, because she called me every day before my alarm went off at four in the morning. It was damn near eleven, and she was wide awake.

"Mom, my dad said that he's outside!" Blossom yelled.

"Don't fuckin' move," I instructed and made my way out the back door.

This nigga had the music blasting so damn loud that the windows on Nana's house were shaking. I didn't even waste my time grabbing my coat, and the cold winter air was smacking me in my face. The snow was picking up and sticking to the ground. I made my way down the driveway with my gun in my hand. Once I made it to the end of the driveway where Mack had parked Honey's truck blocking Nana's driveway, I jumped in the passenger side of the truck.

"What the fuc—" Mack attempted to say but was cut off by the barrel of my gun going down his throat, knockin' out the front row of his teeth.

Mack screamed out in pain, but nobody could see but me and him with this dark ass tint on this truck. Every car that Honey had ever had, she had to have tint. The smell of this nigga's dirt weed mixed with stale ass cigarettes was making my eyes burn.

"You're a disrespectful ass nigga. My sister doesn't even smoke, and you're smoking in her shit," I spat.

Tears filled this niggas eyes, but he could save them bitches, because the only thing that was stoppin' me from sending this nigga to his maker was his daughters. Honey could get over it, but even though they light-skinned, bald, Phil and Lil from the *Rugrats* lookin' asses got on my nerves, I wouldn't want to put them through that.

"Where the fuck are the keys to my sister's house?" I asked once I got sick of hearing this nigga whine.

He pointed toward the arm rest. I pushed the button, opening the armrest, and took out Honey's truck keys and saw a few keys that could have been her house keys and slipped them into my pocket.

"Don't go back to my sister's house. If you want to see your kids, then call them, and they'll call me, and I'll bring them to see you. If you go anywhere near my muthafuckin sister, well nigga, you know how this is goin' to go," I said and reached around him, opening his door and pushing his soft ass out.

"Man, I'll do whatever you say, but can you just give me my keys off the key ring?" Mack begged.

"Nigga, what the fuck are the keys to? You don't have shit but the shit that you were able to finesse out of Honey."

"It's my keys to my momma's."

"Then I suggest you call yo' muthafuckin momma and tell that toothless bitch to make you a copy of her key. Get the fuck up! You a bitch ass nigga. You need to get yo' shit together. You're supposed to be a fuckin' example to my nieces on what the fuck a man is supposed to be," I spat as I jumped out the truck and stormed over to the driver side.

Mack struggled to stand on his two feet. This nigga might've been a buck fifty. Honey was bigger than this little nigga. He was a clown; he had all these dreams to make it big in the dope game but couldn't make it past a quarter to save his life. I think the nigga was smoking the dope he claimed he sold, but Honey swore he didn't. Honey always had a thing for light-skinned niggas, and out of all the niggas I knew about, this nigga was the worst. I'd rather her be with a white man than this bitch, and I hated white people.

Mack didn't waste his time sayin' shit else; he made his way down the street. I parked Honey's truck in front of the house and made my way back in through the back door. Honey was still sittin' where I left her at, listening to some sad ass Betty Wright as Nana sang along like somebody broke her heart and she was still not over it. I sat down across from Honey on a bar stool, puttin' her keys on the island that separated us.

I was just tryin' to figure out where the fuck I went wrong with her. As soon as I made enough money, I got her out of the hood. I paid for her to go to a catholic junior high and high school so she could get a better education than the one that me and Gunna had. As long as she kept up her grades, which she did, whatever she wanted, she got. She had a full ride scholarship to play basketball at Duke University, and then she got pregnant with the twins.

With her being pregnant, she had to stop playin' ball, and that shit broke her heart, but she didn't want to get an abortion. I didn't want her to throw away her future with playing ball, but she had to make the decision. She claimed that she still wanted to go to Duke University, so I got her an apartment, sent one of my workers to North Carolina with her, and paid the tuition. After one semester, she was homesick and wanted to come home, so she transferred to Denver University and came back.

Through her entire pregnancy, that nigga Mack was ghost. She didn't tell me the truth about their status until she got back home and broke down cryin' as I opened the door. For months, she had been lying to me tellin' me that they were good and they were tryin' to get prepared for the twins, and the whole time, she didn't even have that nigga's phone number. I always told myself that I would stay out of her shit with him because the more I protested her dealing with that nigga when it was convenient for him, the harder she was goin' to hold on to him.

I stayed out of it unless she brought some shit to me. Even then, I only fixed whatever the fuck that nigga had fucked up and stayed out of their relationship shit. Whatever she needed to make sure that her and the twins were good, for years, I made it happen on the strength of them. I bought the fuckin' house that they lived in. A year ago, when Honey came to me crying and sayin' that he had forged her name on the paperwork and cashed out her trust fund, I was done helping. When Honey looked me in my face and told me that she couldn't leave him, I was done.

The nigga was scared of me, so whenever I was around, he wasn't. I'd probably seen the nigga six times in the ten years that he and Honey had been dealing with each other. Gunna didn't take the same approach that I did when it came to Mack. He had pistol whipped that nigga Mack in front of his momma.

Mack signed the birth certificate for the twins at gunpoint and could barely see out of one of his eyes because Gunna had beat him so bad. No matter how many ass whoopings this nigga got behind how he did Honey, the bullshit just never seemed to stop. Taking her truck and kicking her out her home was where I drew the fucking line. I'd never put my hands on the nigga, and anything that I said to him it was never a conversation; I talked and he listened.

"Did you kill him?" Honey asked, breaking the silence that lingered between us.

"I know ya black ass didn't kill nobody in my damn driveway," Nana spat as she came into the kitchen.

"What you think?" I asked Honey as Nana came around and sat next to me as I tried to help her onto the barstool.

"Nigga, get off of me! I don't need yo' fuckin' help."

"Alright, when ya old ass fall, I don't want to hear none of yo' shit," I replied.

"Girl, naw he didn't. He knows better than to do some bullshit like that at my damn house, hell," Nana replied for me.

"What I want to know is, is your ass really done with this nigga this time? Because I'm gon' be honest with you. I'm sick of you and that muthafucka at this point. Those bald babies deserve better than what the fuck they've been exposed to because you can't let that lil' damn near white boy go. This criminal muthafucka did all types of shit to give you a better life, and ever since you got pregnant, you just been doin' dumb shit. I just don't understand why, and you can't ever seem to answer that question for me.

"But I told you when that nigga took that money from you and bought a house and married that white woman that whatever y'all had was over, and it was only going to get worse. Look at this shit here. That muthafucka claims that he lost the house that he bought just a year ago and kicked you and the twins out so he could move her and her kids into the house that this criminal muthafucka stole, and sold whatever that wasn't chained to the fuckin' ground," Nana said, taking over my damn conversation.

"You don't have to keep callin' me a criminal," I said as soon as Nana took a break from talkin' us to death.

"With a name like Nightmare, what the fuck do you think you are?" Nana asked, turnin' to me, waiting for an answer.

"Honey, go and get some rest. I'll let you know when you can go back to the house," I said, and Honey got up, taking her phone, and turned to leave the kitchen.

"What is she goin' to do when you or my baby Christopher isn't around anymore? Because you two criminal muthafuckas ain't gon' ever get y'all shit together," Nana asked.

"She gon' get her shit together, because after I get that nigga's wife and her kids out that house and get it cleaned, she's goin' to be on her own. I'll do anything for the kids, but I'm tellin' Gunna that we gotta let her figure everything else out on her own. You right; we aren't goin' to always be around, and we can't keep saving her. She doesn't have to worry about that nigga coming back around her, but she is goin' to have to figure out how to make shit happen. She needs to use that fuckin' degree I paid for her ass to get."

"So, what are you waitin' for to get yo' shit together? You and dumb ass Bonnie gon' write each other when y'all both locked up?"

"Nana, quit callin' my baby dumb. She's back on the right track. And why the fuck you always gotta talk shit about a nigga gettin' locked up, damn?"

"The game isn't the same, Nightmare, and you know it. Why not get out while you're ahead? Don't be greedy, because Bonnie can't come and stay here. I'm too damn old to be runnin' to pick her ass up from jail," Nana said.

"Goodnight, Nana," I said, kissin' her on the cheek and getting up to leave.

"Don't kiss me and you out there kissin' them hoes in them streets. And where the fuck are you goin'? You better get ya ass back in here and take out this trash 'fore I turn this into a real fuckin' nightmare!" Nana yelled as I tried to make my way out the kitchen.

I turned around and grabbed the trash and made my way out the back door. I locked the top and bottom lock while Nana stood in the door twisting the door handle, making sure it was locked. I threw the trash into the can on the curb as I read a text from Gunna on my trap phone saying that the baby was pretty, so I knew that the money at all of our spots was right. I saw that Honey texted me, but I didn't open it; I scrolled right past it. Jumpin' in my car, I made my way to Kay's.

It took me about thirty minutes to get to Kay's spot. Pulling into a visitor's parking spot, I made my way inside the building using the code. The building door was unlocked, so I made my way in and down the long hallway to the elevator. I nodded my head as I passed the security guard that was sitting at the front desk. We'd exchanged words, and he ended up having to get fucked up because he thought I was about to give him my damn ID to get in here. It didn't take him long to find out that I didn't give a fuck about the rules or his damn job.

Pressing the button to the top floor, I waited for the elevator to come down. It was quiet as hell in this building— too damn quiet, but Kay damn sure wasn't coming to my house, so over here was the only way I'd see her ass. The elevator finally made it down to the lobby, so I stepped on. A security guard was in the right corner of the spacious elevator. He nodded his head, and I did the same. I stepped on, and the elevator door closed behind me, swiftly making its way up top floor.

When I stepped off, I walked straight into Kay's living room. I could hear some ratchet ass City Girls coming from the speaker that she kept in the kitchen. As I looked down the hall, I didn't hear or see Kay. I made my way over to the couch, sitting down, and I kicked off my shoes and turned on the TV.

Kay made her way in the living room but didn't say anything, just how I liked it. She only tried that wanting to talk shit when she hadn't seen me in a while. I didn't see this bitch for a week, and she turned into Maya Angelou in my text messages. A month, and this bitch started calling back to back, and if I didn't answer, she left messages playing love songs in the background. It had been almost a month, and when she walked around the sectional and made her way in front of me, she dropped to her knees. No asking questions, no bullshit telling me about her day of shopping, no whining about her punk ass daddy or her alcoholic ass momma. Just how I liked it, because if you weren't my bitch, which she wasn't, I didn't give a fuck about none of that shit. The only thing she could do for me was exactly what she was doing right now with her mouth, and because she was doin' this so well, she could have some dick this time.

Chapter Nine

GIONNA "GIA" SIMMONS

taring at his gun, I just wanted this to be over. I didn't know why he had me in this house. Gunna was usually in and out, but for some reason, today he'd been here since I opened my eyes. I just knew that if him or his brother found me, they would kill me on the spot, but they didn't. I hadn't even seen his brother. The fear of the unknown was killin' me, and he wouldn't tell me anything.

Who the hell kidnapped somebody and brought them to a fully furnished home? The only home that I could even compare this place to was my sister's, but this place was more modern than hers. I could tell that a woman was responsible for everything. Niggas weren't into candles, plants, or books, and that shit was in every room.

Ring, ring, ring.

This nigga's phone was always ringing. It was probably just anotha bitch callin' because clearly, he had a lot of those.

"Can you just kill me and get it over with? How fuckin' long do you plan on keeping me here?" I screamed.

"I could be starvin' yo' ass and have you tied up in the fuckin' basement, so if I was you, I'd shut the fuck up and relax," Gunna suggested.

"I've been here for a week. I already told you, I'm not goin' to tell the police shit. I can't stay in this fuckin' house!" I screamed out in between jumpin' up and snatching his gun off the table and putting it to my head with my finger lightly tappin' against the trigger.

"Let me go, or I'll just kill myself. What the fuck do I have to lose? I know y'all done killed my daughter already!" I screamed as the tears I had been holding back fell down my face fast.

"I ain't never heard about a Chinese person killin' they self. Go on 'head do yo' thang because I'm sick of hearing you fuckin' whine," Gunna said and lit his blunt.

"I'm Korean, muthafucka!" I spat, feelin' disrespected.

"Get out my face with that bullshit. If you're not goin' to pull the trigger, go make me some egg rolls," Gunna said, waving me off.

While wiping my tears away with my free hand and weighing my options in my head. As the smoke filled his lungs, he wasted no time blowin' the smoke in my face. He didn't have a care in the fuckin' world. Me being gone wouldn't make him any difference and would just make the task at hand easier. I blamed myself for my daughter's demise. Every night that I was away from her over the past month had been unbearable. I had to stay high and drunk to be able to even cope.

This shit wasn't Kiara's fault. She didn't deserve to be born into this. I was supposed to give her better than I ever had, but how, when I didn't know the first thing about being a mother? I never had a mom to paint my nails, do my hair, or anything that other little girls experienced. My momma made sure that we had food in the house, but that was about it. She used to chase behind my dad, but once he was gone, she found other people to occupy her time.

Fuck it. I'm just goin' to do it.

Closing my eyes, I pulled the trigger, and it clicked, but nothin' happened, so I pulled it again, and again, still nothin'.

"Dumb ass, take the safety off," Gunna said as I opened my eyes, and his smoke went into them.

I started fumbling with the gun, and he jumped up, filled with irritation and snatched the gun from my grasp. He clicked back the safety, staring me in the eyes, and forcefully handed the gun back to me. Staring at the gun and tappin' my foot, I went over my options, and right now this was the only way that I saw me being able to deal with the fact that I put my daughter in harm's way by bringing her into this world.

With the gun in my hand, squeezing it tight and closing my eyes even tighter. The barrel of the gun to my head and tapping the trigger lightly, shaking because I know once I pull the trigger there isn't any going back. I could still feel that

Gunna was standing in front of me even though my eyes were closed.

Fuck it.

Pop!

As I pulled the trigger, something hit my hand, and the gun and me fell to the ground hard. I feel like I have a ton of bricks on my chest. I didn't feel as much pain as I thought I would.

"What the fuck is yo' problem?" Gunna spat as his minty breath hit my face.

"What the fuck are you doin'?" I managed to say, opening my eyes, and Gunna was on top of me.

"You need to be thanking me. I could have let yo' dumb ass kill yo' self," Gunna said, still on top of me, lookin' at me in disgust.

"Get the fuck off of me! You don't know shit about me. Why the fuck haven't y'all just killed me yet? Damn!" I screamed.

"Why the fuck do you want to die so bad?" Gunna asked as he got up off of me.

He reached out to lend me a hand. I left his hand hangin' as I got up off the floor. Lookin' up at the ceiling, I saw the hole that the bullet left.

"You want somethin' to eat?" Gunna asked and waited for an answer.

I didn't waste my time responding. Every day he asked the same thing, and every day, I didn't answer, but he still got me somethin' to eat. My stomach was growlin', and it was so damn loud I knew he could hear it. I walked out of the dining room and made my way to the living room. Gunna was on my heels but hadn't said anything.

"Don't you have somethin' better to do?" I asked as I plopped down on the couch, runnin' my fingers through my hair.

***

Rubbin' my eyes, I looked over, and Gunna was still here, talkin' loud as hell on the phone with a bitch. Lookin' at the clock, it was eight in the mornin'. I damn sure didn't plan on sleeping that long. I stretched, and my stomach started growlin' loud as hell. This nigga was in a whole new outfit and was ready for the day. As soon as he looked over at me, I rolled my eyes, and he abruptly ended his call because the bitch was still bumpin' her gums loud as hell. I could hear everything she was sayin' loud and clear.

"When is the last time you got yo' hair and nails done? You out here lookin' bad," Gunna said, staring at me from across the room.

"Why the fuck do you care?" I asked and looked down at my nails.

My hair was all over my head, and on my left hand I was missin' one nail, and on the right, I was missin' two, and one was broken. Since the day I'd left Kiara at the hospital with Milan, it had been rough. The last thing on my mind was my appearance. Every day, this nigga had somethin' to say about it. It was usually the first thing he said to me, but I didn't understand why.

"No woman is supposed to ever leave the house without their hair done," Gunna said as somebody knocked on the door.

"What am I doin' my hair for, my funeral?" I asked as Gunna made his way to open the door.

"I never met somebody so obsessed with death. You one of them bitches that sit in the house watching the ID Channel all day?" he asked as he opened the door.

"Black ass, took you fuckin' long enough," Gunna said as he opened the door, and this girl came storming in the house.

"Why the fuck are you way out here? And who is this girl that got you willing to pay me to drive all the fuck way out here?" the woman asked as she turned and looked at me.

"Get her together. I'm sick of lookin' at her lookin' like this," Gunna said, taking a stack of money out of his pockets and handin' it to the lady.

Gunna made his way over to the couch that I was sittin' on and sat too close to me. He wrapped his arm around me, and he smelled so good; I can't even lie. Gunna pulled my face close to his, and he was making me uncomfortable. Him or none of his people had tried anything, so I didn't think now he would.

"Get yo' hair and shit done and do it with a fuckin' smile. Don't say the wrong thing, or I will have to go and get yo' momma a fuckin' black dress." Gunna whispered in my ear, causing chills to cover my body.

"Got it, sweetheart?" he asked, but I still didn't say anything.

I snatched away from his grasp, and he quickly grabbed me and held me tight.

"I been being cool, but if you want this shit to go another way, it can. Because I know that you don't want me to play with a gun," Gunna said as he held me tight.

"Alright, you can get some pussy after I'm done. I need to get her done and get back to civilization," the lady said, grabbin' my arm to pull me up off the couch.

"Girl, you must got some fire. His ass won't pay for me to come to travel to anybody," the woman sang as she led the way to the back of the house.

As I followed her, I didn't even know that this room existed. I'd never even been back here. There hadn't been any reason for me to come back here. It was a whole damn hair salon. I didn't know why the fuck he was doin' any of this. This house was literally in the middle of nowhere. I'd thought about tryin' to run, but I didn't even know where the fuck I would be runnin' to.

"What's your name? You can call me Black. I'm Gunna's cousin, not one of the dumb bitches," Black said as she put a cape on me so she could wash my hair.

"Gia," I replied as she washed my hair.

"Gia, I haven't ever seen you before. Where did you meet my cousin?"

"Girl, you know, just around," I said, hoping she cut the twenty-one questions.

With her being his cousin, she damn sure wasn't goin' to help me in any way, so I wouldn't waste my time asking her for help. But to be honest, it wasn't like I had shit to risk. What the fuck did I have to live for? My daughter was gone, and the only man that made sure that I was good and had cared anything about me was gone too. The only other person that I had that cared about me was Milan, but I couldn't take her judgement right now.

"Girl, I haven't been to this house in years. The fact that he brought you here says a lot," Black suggested.

I didn't even respond, because she didn't know that it meant nothin'. As she washed my hair, I tried to relax, but that wasn't happening. With all the stress that I was under, that wasn't workin'. My shoulders had been so damn tight that just sittin' down hurt, and being in this chair wasn't helping any. I closed my eyes as she washed my hair because this shit felt so good. It had been so long since I'd had somebody else wash my hair.

"So, where y'all goin'?" Black asked.

"Black, why the fuck you always askin' so many damn questions? Just do the fuckin' job you were paid to do. I don't know who the fuck charges their family them prices. Shit, if you want to start smokin', I'd give you a family eight ball," Gunna said.

I couldn't get a full ten minutes without him or one of his workers all in my face.

"Fuck yo' big ass. You don't ever have to worry 'bout givin' me no family discounts. I don't give a fuck who you are; you payin' full prices, and if you inconvenience me in any way, you're payin' for my next bag," Black said as she dried my hair off with the towel.

"Why wouldn't you tell me that her hair was blonde?" Black asked.

"What the fuck difference does it make?" Gunna asked.

"Umm, a lot, fat ass. Girl, I'll be right back, I need to see if I have somethin' close to this color in my car," Black said and disappeared.

For a few minutes, Gunna and I were just having a staring contest, but this nigga was smiling like somethin' was funny. He was always fuckin' smiling, and that shit pissed me off. Who the fuck was always happy? Nobody but this nigga for sure.

"Where are we goin'?" I asked.

"Does it matter? You want to die so bad, so I'm gon' take yo' ass to pick out a casket," Gunna said.

"So, what am I wearing?" I asked.

"A bad ass dress I had my bitch Nikki go get," Gunna replied.

"So, you have a bitch that would go and get another female clothes?"

"Girl, them bitches will go and play in traffic during rush hour if this nigga says to," Black said as she came back in the room.

"You better be lucky that I had this hair, with yo' stupid ass," Black said as she hit Gunna in the face with the bundles.

"Uttt unn, where did you get that shit from? I see fuckin'

threads. That's some used shit. What I paid for that shit, it needs to come out the fuckin' wrap like some dope!" Gunna spat.

"I had to cut it out this bitch's head. Long story, but it's new. She didn't even have it in her head for long."

"Naw, I want some of my fuckin' money back!"

"Boy, fuck you. You not getting shit back," Black said, waving me over to the chair.

"Ain't nothin' worse than a cheap drug dealer," I said, catchin' Gunna off guard. His mouth dropped open.

"I like her. She talks shit back. None of them bitches do that. You gon' be this nigga's wife. You the one," Black assured me.

"Is she?" Gunna asked.

"Yeah, because them dumb bitches don't talk back, and you don't respect 'em. So she the one. They scared of yo' big ass," Black said and then started blow drying my hair.

Gunna was chunky, light skinned, and had this mean mug if he wasn't laughin' and talkin' shit. I knew who he was way before this shit happened. Everybody knew who he was. Him and his brother were well known. I hadn't met a bitch that didn't drool by the sight of them, so the fact that he had all these bitches it doesn't surprise me.

Every nigga wanted to be them, and every bitch just wanted one chance to even talk to them. Gunna was a friendly ass nigga, so he'd talk to damn near anybody. Nightmare was anotha story; that nigga didn't even speak if he didn't fuck with you. They were like night and day, and that would explain the way that Gunna treated me. Because if Nightmare was here, I'd be chained to a fuckin' chair being tortured. Clearly, Gunna liked to kill females slow and wined and dined them before the kill.

It took about an hour, and Black had got my hair together. She handed me a mirror, and I looked at my hair briefly. I looked over at Gunna, and he was staring at me. Black spun my chair around.

"What the fuck is wrong with you? Because I know that I'm cold, and anybody else would be pulling out their phone to take a selfie. So what the fuck is goin' on?"

"Nothin'. I'm good," I assured her, but my face said it all.

"She good," Gunna replied for me.

"Just finish doin' yo' fuckin' job," Gunna said and made his way out the room.

She shrugged her shoulders and opened up a box full of makeup.

"Utt, unn. You can leave this part out," I said, not wanting no parts.

I'm not 'bout to be walkin' 'round this bitch lookin' like a clown, even if I am living on borrowed time. I don't wear makeup and never have; I don't need it. The only thing that my momma gave me was this skin, and I have never had a pimple in my life.

"Now, I like you, but I was given specific instructions for your look. I don't like you enough to come up off any of this money. So just sit back and let a real nigga get you together.

Because you're beautiful, but you were in this bitch lookin' like nobody loves you," Black suggested.

I sat back in the chair and let her do her thing because I respected her grind and nothin' else. She assured me that I was safe in her hands, and she wasn't goin' to have me lookin' like a clown. I really wanted to know why he was doin' all this. I really didn't understand. I could smell Gunna's cologne, so I know that he was back in the room, even with my eyes closed.

About thirty minutes passed, and Black was done. She tried to hand me the mirror, but I declined. I didn't want to see this shit. I liked it better when his worker was here watching me. He didn't say shit to me, and I didn't say shit to him. It was quiet, and I was left alone with my thoughts and fucked-up reality. She cut down my nails and removed the ones I had still hangin' on by a thread. Then she proceeded to get them together, and I had to admit, she was cold at this too.

"How long have you been doing hair and nails?" I asked.

"Shit, since I was thirteen. Gunna made all his bitches be my models while I was getting my license a few years ago. That's when the price went up. Bitches had been playin' forever, not wanting to pay me what the fuck I was worth, but Gunna made me go to school after my momma passed away. Every day, he would pick me up in the morning and take me to and from school. Shit, the first few days, he stayed just to make sure I wouldn't leave.

"He talks his shit, but he has a good heart. Even for muthafuckas he should have made swim with the fishes. Don't get it twisted; that fuckin' teddy bear will turn into a fuckin' grizzly. He stands tall when it's time and will let that bitch blow until the clip's empty," Black assured me, and I glanced back at Gunna who was doin' something on his phone.

Black finished up my nails, and I was sittin' under a light as they dry. I glanced back, and Gunna was just staring at me. He was nothin' like I imagined him to be. Shit, up until I was forced to come here, I'd never even had a conversation with him. I'd just seen him around, and he was always around. He wasn't scared to walk around in the hood, or shit, post up on the block. But that is what makes him such a target for niggas out here.

"Alright, y'all have fun, and I'll be back in a week," Black said as she made her way out the room, leaving me and Gunna.

"A week? So you think that I'm about to keep doin' this bullshit for anotha week?" I asked.

"Shit, we don't gotta stop there. What would you rather be doin'?" he asked.

"Gunna, I get it. You're not as reckless as I assumed, but this is all too much. I really don't see a reason for you to be doing all this."

"I get it. You never had nobody do nothin' for you. So you not used to this shit, but this really ain't shit, and considering the situation how we met, you could be a little more grateful."

"What the fuck should I be grateful for, that my kidnapper called his cousin out here to do my hair? Thank you! Thank you so much! How could I ever repay you?" I asked, jumpin' up and standin' in front of him praisin' him.

"Kiss my muthafuckin Js. Take these bitches off and rub a nigga's feet while you're at it," he suggested.

"Kiss my ass!" I spat.

"I would if you would just shut the fuck up," he said, catchin' me off guard.

"Go upstairs, wash yo' ass, and get dressed. Don't take all fuckin' day. We got reservations," he said and got up from his seat.

Chapter Ten

MILAN

Rollin' over in my hotel room, my phone was ringin', but I didn't waste my time answering it. I didn't feel like talking. My work phone was powered off, and I needed some me time. I left my house because I got sick of Ervin thinking that he could just pop up whenever the fuck he felt like it.

He was not making this easy, and to be honest, I was not even surprised. He wanted me to break down and just give in and take him back. After showing up to the house drunk and beggin' me to open the door several times, my attorney advised me of what he was offering. After a month of the back and forth, I was already exhausted. I didn't know how much of this I was goin' to be able to take.

I'd been working ten-hour days Mondays through Thursdays, just to be able to get an extra day off to just relax. I still didn't understand why a man that I was everything he wanted me to be and gave him all of me, wanted me to suffer when he was the one that fucked up. If anything, he should've just wanted me to be happy and to go on with my life, but I guess that was asking for too much.

Knock, knock, knock.

Who could that be? I didn't order any room service, and nobody knows that I'm staying here. I rolled over and just stared out the window, and they knocked again.

"Wrong room!" I yelled out, and they just kept on knockin'.

I threw on my robe and made my way through the suite to the door.

"You must have the wrong room," I said as I swung the door open.

"Naw, I got the right room," Maurice said and brushed past me, making his way in the room.

"Maurice, why are you here?"

"Why are you here, is my question," he said as he got comfortable on the couch, kickin' his feet up.

"How can I help you, Maurice? Is everything okay with Amayah?"

"Yeah, she's good. Have you eaten breakfast?"

"Maurice—"

"I asked you a yes or no question, and you can stop sayin' my damn name."

"No."

He reached over and grabbed the phone off the table next to him and snatched the menu up too.

"Don't get excited. You payin' for yo' own shit," he threw in, making me roll my eyes.

I pulled the rope on my robe tighter. I didn't have on any clothes, and he was sittin' here in my room ordering breakfast. I had been seeing him a lot lately, and a lot of the times when I saw him, I wasn't on the clock. Amayah had been inviting me over every other day it seemed like for dinner. I think she just wanted me there so he wouldn't make her eat peanut butter and jelly, but because I didn't have anything else better to do, I'd been goin'.

Whenever I was around them, Amayah was tryin' to convince us that we should date. He never said anything, and I always politely declined. There was no way that I could even entertain anyone right now. I needed to get this situation with Ervin in my rearview before I even considered dating. Not to mention that Maurice's attitude was an acquired taste, and I didn't think that it was somethin' that I could deal with on a regular basis.

"Why would you hang up without letting me order what I wanted?" I asked.

"I ordered for you. You're at my damn house every other day. I know what the fuck you like," he insisted.

I didn't waste my time sayin' anything.

"Go put some clothes on," he spat.

"You can leave because I didn't invite you here."

"I don't repeat myself to nobody but old people and kids, so I suggest that you—"

I stormed out the room and made my way to the bathroom and threw on the jogging suit that I had planned on wearing today so he would just chill and get to why the hell he was here.

"So, you just walk around with no draws on?" he asked.

"Maurice, please get to why you're here. I'm really not in the mood to be questioned right now."

"Yo' pussy must be dry, because ain't no way that you should be able to have on them joggin' pants and no draws."

"The moistness between my legs wouldn't be any of your business."

"Yeah, that muthafucka dry."

I made my way back to the bathroom and turned on the shower so I could get in. My pussy was far from dry, and the sight of him had my juices drippin', and I was surprised that it didn't start drippin' down my legs when I had on the robe. I didn't know what it is about him that made my body have this reaction to him, but I knew that it wasn't good. Even though me and Ervin were definitely done, I was still married, and he was still my client's father.

Once the water was hot, I got in and got myself together since I was being forced to put on panties. This was not what I had in mind for the weekend. Once I was showered and with the proper undergarments to avoid having a discussion with Maurice, I made my way out the bathroom.

After about twenty minutes more of Maurice questioning

me, they came up with our food. He definitely had been payin' attention and made the correct choice for my breakfast. His phone started ringing, and he glanced at it, silenced it, and slipped it back in his pocket.

"When is the last time you had some dick?" he asked, staring at me.

"What?" I asked, even though I heard him loud and clear.

My phone started ringing, and I didn't even get up to check it and see who it is. He waited for me to, but I just kept eating, ignoring it like I was ignoring his question.

"I know that you can hear, but I know it's been a minute. What, is it cobwebs down there or somethin'?"

"No," I said, and I couldn't help but laugh.

My phone started ringing again, and this time I looked at it, but I didn't recognize the number, so I was sure it was Ervin, so I just silenced it. Looked across the table at Maurice, and he was just looking at me.

"So, why aren't you married? I'm sure there is a lot of women who would love to be with you."

Maurice didn't answer my question; he finished eating his breakfast like I hadn't said anything. I didn't get him; he could ask me a million questions and expected an answer to all of them promptly, but this nigga would never answer my questions. A few minutes passed, and Maurice had finished his breakfast.

He got up from the table and set down the money for his food. He headed to the door, so I got up and followed behind him. He opened the door and made his way out but stopped and turned back to look at me once he was out the room.

"Be at the airport next Thursday at ten a.m.," he suggested.

"For?"

"Be at the airport. Bring yo' passport, and don't pack none of them big ass granny panties you got on," he insisted and then just walked away.

"These aren't granny panties!" I yelled out in frustration.

"Tell everybody in the damn hotel you got on granny panties, den," Maurice suggested, turnin' around to face me.

***

I was tryin' to find some patience, but finding a house had become a pain. I had seen so many places, but all the ones that I really liked were in the same neighborhood that I lived in with Ervin. I didn't want to live over there, but some of these other places in other areas didn't even come close to comparing. My realtor was running late, and I was trying to be understanding, but the way my time was set up, I didn't have time to wait.

My phone started ringing, and it was Maurice. I sent him to voicemail, and my phone started ringing right away, and it was a number I didn't recognize. I hesitated, but I answered it, and it was Jeremey, Ervin's coworker.

"I know that you're dealing with your own issues. I can only imagine, but I was wondering if you can testify on my behalf for my divorce proceedings?" Jeremy asked, wasting no time.

"Jeremy, I really don't want to get involved. Like you said, I'm goin' through my own stuff, and I'm sorry, but I really can't help you."

"Well, I'll just give you time to think about it," he replied.

"That, won't be—"

Tap, tap, tap.

"I have to go," I said and hung up on him while holdin' my chest because somebody was tappin' on my window.

I couldn't see who it was behind the tint, but they scared the hell out of me. I took a deep breath and got myself together while my heart was about to beat out of my chest.

"Why would you think it would be okay for you to send me to voicemail?" Maurice asked as I rolled down the window.

"I'm sorry, Maurice, but you must have me confused with someone else. You don't pay Sprint every month; I do. So I don't have to answer my phone when anybody calls me if I don't want to."

Maurice made his way over to the passenger side without replying and tried to open the door that was locked.

"So what, I gotta pay your car note to sit in your car too?" he asked.

"I don't have a car note," I advised him while unlocking the doors.

"Why are you so damn scary? It's broad daylight, and you

got the doors locked like you're in the hood and not in the suburbs."

"What difference does it make to you, Maurice? How did you even know where I was at? You can't just be poppin' up on me like this."

"Why are you looking for a house? What was wrong with where you were staying?"

"I had to get my place ready to be sold, so I put all my belongings in storage so it could be set up for an open house. It should be selling any day now, so I need to find a new place."

"Why are you over here? It's some nicer places over by my house."

"Well thanks for the information, Maurice."

"You got a smart-ass mouth."

I laughed because I couldn't believe that he would have the audacity to say anyone had a smart mouth; he talks so much shit all the time. He was so serious, but I just had to let it go. He sat in the car with me while I waited for my realtor to arrive at the property, offering me his unsolicited opinions about housing options that were available.

I didn't know how much money he thought I made, but there was no way that I could afford any of the stuff that he was suggesting. I hoped that things worked out in my favor with my divorce, but I couldn't make decisions based on hopes. Either way it went, I needed to be able to cover my own ass.

I was tryin' to figure out what Maurice's angle was. Why

was he just poppin' up on me all of a sudden? Why was he tryin' to get me to go out of the country with him? Not too long ago, I was the police, and he didn't even want me around, but now all of a sudden, he wanted to make suggestions about my underwear and where I should live.

About twenty minutes passed, and Kelly finally pulled into the driveway of the home that I'd be seeing today.

"Okay, well this is my realtor, so I guess I'll see you some other time," I said as I went to get out of my car.

I made my way over to the house as Kelly jumped out of her car. I turned back to hit the locks on my car, and Maurice was right behind me. I didn't say anything because I didn't want to cause a scene in front of Kelly. I hit the locks on my car as Kelly tried to introduce herself to Maurice. But of course, he had to be an ass.

"Who shows up late to show a property?" Maurice asked, as if she had inconvenienced

him.

"Maurice, no. Not right now," I insisted, and he didn't even acknowledge or look at me.

His tone made Kelly uncomfortable, and her pale skin was turning red. I'd known Kelly for a few years. I met her through Ervin. She helped him get a few rental properties. I hoped that Maurice didn't scare her off.

"I'm sorry. I already apologized to Milan. I had some issues with the closing of her property," Kelly pleaded, tryin' to calm Maurice.

"Kelly, you're fine," I assured her and gave her the floor to show me the home.

As we went from room to room, Kelly's confidence was all gone, and she was uncomfortable as hell, stuttering and stumbling over her words. Maurice was really pissing me off. He was asking more questions than me. I can't lie; he was very knowledgeable, and this was definitely his lane. He was asking questions that I never would have asked; I was concerned about cosmetic stuff. He was asking questions about plumbing, structure, and heating. While I was concerned about the kitchen cabinets and thinking about the countertops, Maurice was asking questions that were far more important.

"I'll just give you guys some time to look around on your own," Kelly said and excused herself.

She was embarrassed as hell, and Maurice had done his normal thing and belittled the hell out of her.

"Maurice, you're out of line. I didn't ask you for your help. I'm sure Kelly no longer wants to work with me. Thanks for trying to help, but you're not helping by insulting my realtor and interrogating her," I whispered once Kelly was out of the room.

My phone vibrated in my pocket. I pulled it out, and it was an unknown number, but with the preview of the message, I knew that it's Ervin threatening me about selling the house. It was too late; I was doing it, so I'd just take my chances. I couldn't live in the house that I was supposed to be in with him, and he should've understood that. Not to mention, he had a family around the corner.

"You worried about the color of the appliances and shit. This is her lane; she shouldn't be uncomfortable about me asking questions about the important shit. Don't buy this fuckin' house. I got some people that I can hook you up with that can get some shit built from the ground for what you're goin' to pay for this old ass house. Your goin' to end up spending way more than that buying this house. The water heater and boiler are on their last fuckin' leg," Maurice said, slippin' his hands in his jean pockets.

"Can you just go?"

"I'm not," he spat, standing his ground.

I rolled my eyes and made my way back around the home with Maurice on my heels. He clearly wasn't leaving, even though I have asked him to. I had enough goin' on, and the last thing I needed was a man that wasn't mine tryin' to make me follow his lead. Tryin' to find my independence was hard enough when I was so used to being able to lean on Ervin. I was not discussing my business with Maurice, so we'd just have to talk once I got rid of Kelly.

After I made my way through the house again, I made my way to the foyer where Kelly was waiting and doing something on her phone. Once she noticed me and Maurice, she jumped up from the stairs, giving us her undivided attention.

"Milan, what are you thinking?" Kelly asked.

"She's not interested," Maurice replied.

"Okay, well I have a few other listings that I can send to you, but I know that you are eager to find something soon. I also know that there is a certain area that you don't want to be by. Have your needs and wants changed?" Kelly asked.

"Ye—" Maurice went to answer, but I cut him off.

"I'll be in touch soon," I assured her.

She breathed hard, and I had to pull Maurice by his hand to get him out the house so Kelly didn't hear any more of his nonsense. He was still talkin' shit, but I held his hand tight as I made my way to the street. If he wanted to snatch away from me and go and tell Kelly everything he was sayin' to her face, he could have easily. Luckily, he didn't.

At first, I was starting to get intrigued by Maurice and some of his antics, but now I was just annoyed. He was out of line and causing a strain between me and a realtor. Even though he brought up some great points and had changed some of original requirements for my future home, the way that he was goin' about it is all wrong and rude as hell.

"Get in my truck," Maurice said as I let go of his hand.

"I'm not. Are you crazy?" I asked, even though I knew the answer.

He blocked me from getting into my car, giving me the answer to my question as Kelly looked on from the porch. He snatched my keys from my hand, and I breathed hard, and he didn't care or wasn't fazed at all. Maurice led the way to his truck and opened the passenger side door for me to get in. Once I was in, he closed the door and made his way over to the driver's side door and got in.

As he pulled away from the curb, he asked Siri to call somebody and took his phone off of Bluetooth as he talked to some woman. He was so calm and collected, and I was pissed, not that he cared. I just wanted to go back to my car so I could go to the hotel. I pulled out my phone, and I had an email from Kelly telling me that someone else was making an offer for my house. Because of the amount, I knew that somehow Ervin was behind it, so I quickly emailed her back and declined.

I was sure she was pissed because of the amount of money she would make off the deal, but I didn't care. If I didn't need to sell the house, I would just keep it to ensure he would never be able to get it, but I needed a place to live. I refused to pay a mortgage payment for rent. The hotel bill was already doing that, and I knew that I couldn't do that for much longer. Kelly quickly advised me to sleep on it, so I didn't even waste my time replying.

"Maurice, where are we going?" I asked as soon as he ended his call.

"Just sit back and relax," he quickly replied.

"I have stuff that I need to do. I don't have time to play this game with you."

"What, go and buy some more granny panties? I told you not to bring none of that shit with you tomorrow."

"I'm not going nowhere with you."

The way he looked at me told me that he thought differently, even with him not saying a word. How the hell was I going to go out of the country with him and Amayah? I didn't have a roof over my head. I rubbed my hands over my face, trying to calm myself down. I sat back and tried to relax, but I couldn't. Meanwhile, he was so calm, and if he was stressing or worried about anything, I would never know.

After about twenty minutes of silence, we made our way to his neighborhood, and I instantly got even more frustrated. I didn't say anything, even though I wanted to go off. I quickly went to my Uber app and ordered a ride from his house, and it was ten minutes away. I didn't have anything else to say to Maurice because at this point, I'd just be wasting my time. As soon as the car came to a stop, I snatched off my seat belt, and he followed suit.

"My realtor is in the house waiting to meet with you. She's solid and knowledgeable. She's worried about getting what you want as well as making sure the home is what you need. You're not supposed to rush when buying a house. It takes time to find the right fit.

"So, just go in here and tell her everything that you need, and she can make sure that you get all of that. Stay within your budget, and get a place that you won't have to dump a bunch of money in within the next few years."

"No, thank you," I said and went to grab the door handle to get out the truck, and he quickly locked the doors.

"I know that a nigga or two done you wrong and led you in the wrong directions, but I'm trying to help you," he insisted.

"I didn't ask for yo' help."

"Sometimes you just need to shut the fuck up and take help when it's being offered. Why the fuck would I fuck you over or do you wrong? What the fuck would I get out of that?"

"Look, Maurice, I don't understand why all of a sudden you want to help me, but regardless of your reasons... Thank you, but no thank—" I said, but was cut off by him kissing me.

Maurice pushed his tongue, not too fast or to slow, into my mouth. As our tongues intertwined, I felt somethin' that I'd never felt before. Maurice wasted no time scooping me up with ease and sitting me on his lap, not breaking our kiss. I tried to break our kiss, but Maurice held onto me tight, and my strength was no match for his.

I tried again, and he grabbed a handful of my hair, not too rough but not gentle, showing me that he was in charge of this interaction whether I wanted him to be or not. A few minutes had passed, and we were still kissin' with passion that I had never experienced. Maurice pulled back, breaking our kiss.

"Go in the house and do what I told you to do, Mrs. Officer," Maurice said calmly, but I knew that he was serious. Then my phone went off.

From the alert noise, I knew it was my Uber arriving.

"I'm n—" I attempted to say, and Maurice took the words right out of my mouth with his tongue again.

"Ohhhhhhh! Yessssss! I knew it was gon' happen!" I heard a familiar voice loudly screech, making me pull away from Maurice.

When I looked back and saw Amayah, I was so damn embarrassed. I had to turn quickly back around and bury my face into Maurice's chest. I looked up at him, and he had the same expression that he always had. He was always mean muggin'. I had never seen him smile, laugh, or not look so damn serious, not even times when everyone around him was having a good time.

"Maurice, this really isn't necessary or appropriate. Your daughter is my client," I said as he opened the door and scooped me up and proceeded to carry me in the house as my Uber pulled up.

"You called a fuckin' Uber?" he asked.

"Utt unn, you carrying her too? Milan, what y'all been doing? I ain't never seen my dad with nobody," Amayah cooed from behind us.

As Maurice carried me through the house, I asked him to put me down a few times and then just gave up because clearly that wasn't goin' to happen. I looked back at Amayah, and she was just so excited and happy. I smiled at her, but I really didn't want her to get her hopes up about this. I was not in the position to even consider entertaining Maurice in any way. His persistence and take-charge capabilities were definitely something that made him difficult to ignore or forget but, it was just not right.

"Well, hi," a beautiful, light-skinned woman said as we entered the sitting room she was waiting in.

"Hi," I said as Maurice set me down on the couch.

"I'm April, and Maurice tells me that you are searching for a home. He gave me a description of some of the things you are looking for, but if you could just elaborate," April requested.

"What did Maurice tell you?" I asked as he and Amayah made their way out the room.

April pulled out her phone and went over her notes from Maurice, and I was impressed. In between him taking over with Kelly while she was showing us the house, he was on his phone on and off, but I surely didn't think that he was communicating with his realtor. Everything that I wanted, Maurice had told her. I only needed to fill April in on the things that I'd never discussed in front of him.

April was very professional but still personable. Anybody that could handle Maurice and his attitude would have to be. I couldn't even imagine how he attempted to handle her. As April and I talked, she pulled out her iPad and began to show me some beautiful homes. She showed me some up and coming developments that would be available in the next few months.

I can't lie; I was blown away by her presentation, but there was no way that I can live in a hotel for a few months. Some of the homes that she showed me that were available now, there was no way that I could afford them off of my salary. We talked for about an hour, and I addressed my concerns. She let me know that she would find the right place for me, within my budget. My mind traveled off to Kelly. I couldn't just dismiss her because Maurice had introduced me to his realtor.

I let April know my dilemma, and she understood and just let me know that she would love to help me, but to just let her know once I made my decision. I assured her I would, and Maurice came back in the room like he knew that we were done talking. Maurice and April briefly talked, and then he walked her to the door while I sat in the sitting room and tried to wrap my head around what happened between Maurice and I.

I didn't want to read into it too much. I tended to think too much, and I didn't want to assume anything about what his intentions were. It could've been as simple as he made it seem, that he was just trying to help. But him kissing me the way he did had my mind going a mile a minute. This could get messy, and I didn't need that right now in my life. I couldn't take any more drama, and I was sure with the little that I knew about Maurice, he didn't need any more issues either.

I'd never asked, and he surely never offered any information about the reason the government would be investigating him. I had a few assumptions, but I didn't have any proof. He could talk business, but he didn't hide the street that was in him. With ease, he could switch it up when time permitted. I'd seen the way that he talked to Amayah's lawyer, the judge over her case, and other professionals, but the way that he handled me today with Kelly was another side of him.

"What did you think about April?" Maurice asked as he came back in the room sitting down next to me on the couch.

"She was cool," I said, tryin' to play it cool.

The truth was she was good. She knew her shit. Every question that I asked, she had an answer for. Every concern, she had a solution. I knew that I had to have a place to live, and I knew that I didn't have much time. I didn't have any family that I would even fix my mouth to ask if I could stay with them. The money that I was going to get from selling the house was going to be a good amount of money, but I still had other expenses to consider. My cell phone vibrated, and I pulled it out. It was an invoice from my attorney. I didn't even want to think about that right now, so I slipped my phone back into my purse and gave my attention back to Maurice.

"I know that she's dope as fuck, so I don't give a fuck what you talkin' 'bout. What's up? What's the issue?" he asked.

"Honestly, I'm just tryin' to wrap my head around this. First, you show up to my hotel, come in, and eat breakfast, and make demands for stuff that I never even knew that you noticed. Then, you just conveniently are in the neighborhood when I'm lookin' at a house, act an ass, and demand that I get in your truck because you set up a meeting with your realtor. Then the kiss," I said, biting my lip as thoughts of the kiss invaded my mind.

Maurice was just lookin' at me but hadn't said anything, and it was pissin' me off. Even though I shouldn't, I felt guilty about even sitting here with Maurice now. My marriage was done, and even though I thought it would take me longer to get over it, I knew that we would never be able to reconcile. But I knew that Maurice and I crossing the line could cause a lot of issues if things didn't work out. I really cared about Amayah, and I didn't want to hurt her or bring any more inconsistency in her life.

"What's the problem?" Maurice asked, taking me away from my thoughts.

"I don't think this is a good idea. I mean, what if—"

"Just sit back and relax. You thinking too damn much about shit that doesn't matter. I'll take you to the room so you can get yo' bag. You can just stay here tonight so you don't have to worry about being on time to the airport in the morning."

"I can't—"

"You're going with us?" Amayah asked as she came running in the room full force.

"Dad! Why didn't you tell me?" Amayah asked, jumpin' on the other side of him and huggin' him tight.

"Come on, Milan. Let me show you my clothes," Amayah said, pulling my hand to get me off the couch.

My phone vibrated, and I had to answer as Amayah led the way up to her room. It was the detective that was working on finding my niece.

Chapter Eleven

GUNNA

I watched Gia as we ate dinner, glancing every so often at the baby that was sitting at the table across from us. From the first time I laid eyes on Gia, I wanted her, and I knew the risk that I would be takin', but shit, in this game, I took risks every time I lifted my head off my pillow. Nightmare wanted her dead, but I knew when I saw her that I couldn't do it. I remembered what the fuck it was like to grow up without my parents, and I couldn't do that to her daughter that she thought was dead. If Nightmare had it his way, he wanted the baby dead too, but it was not goin' to happen.

Gia was beautiful, and I had never met anybody like her before. Her chinky eyes and attitude did somethin' to a nigga. She had a baby face and some chunky cheeks. Shit, she had more tattoos than I had. She had a sleeve that started from her shoulder and went all the way down to her hand. She even had tattoos on her fingers and a few others that were scattered here and there. She didn't have much ass and had a handful of titties, but everything else made up for that.

I had some bitches that could turn heads and an ass that would make every nigga that they passed look back that needed a face full of makeup to feel confident. But Gionna didn't need that. What really made a nigga want to lock her ass up and never let her go was the fact that she spoke her mind. I didn't know if it was because she wanted to be dead so bad or if it was because she really wasn't scared, but I planned to find out soon.

With the picture that Amayah had just sent me of her, Nightmare, and Milan in Mexico, I knew that he'd eventually get over it. I was runnin' shit the way that I saw fit. Gia wasn't going to testify against us, so he didn't have any worries on that end. That was all that he should be worried about. Anything else, I'd handle.

"Can we go?" Gia asked, but not with her usual attitude.

"Go where?" I asked as I watched Gia play with her food while I ate mine.

"To hell already. This is too much. Who goes out to eat three times a day? You are just doing too much. Don't you have other shit that you need to be doing? Where are all those girls that you have at? I'm sick of pretending with you. Going to the movies and doing all this other shit.

"Do you know what it's like for me to see other people out with their kids? Did you consider how the fuck this was making me feel, considering when your brother finds out that I'm still breathing, he's going to kill me, and he's seen my sister, so she's probably going to be next. I really don't want to be here. Can you just get your food to go? Please," Gia whispered.

I didn't like leftovers, so I'd be leaving when I was done eating. She was worried about shit that she didn't need to be worried about. Her sister damn sure wasn't at risk of getting taken out, considering she was on vacation with the nigga. But I needed her to be on her toes and worried about all the possibilities, so when I gave her this ultimatum, she could take all of that shit into consideration.

"I need to go to the bathroom," Gia lied.

I knew when she was lying because she twisted her lips to the left after she lied. I ignored her because she knew that was not an option. She was not going into a bathroom in a public place. Even though I was feelin' her, it wasn't enough to risk her talkin' to nobody but Jesus without me knowing about it. I finished eating my food and laid down money on the table to cover the bill. As we made our way out of Pappadeaux Seafood, my phone vibrated in my pocket. As I pulled it out, I saw it was Nikki.

I slipped it back in my pocket. She was not goin' anywhere, and when I called her, she'd answer before it could ring once good. So I was not worried about her ass and never had to be. Gia walked in front of me with an attitude. She always had an attitude, and I never met somebody that was so obsessed with dying in my life. We could be watching TV, and the characters were getting married, and she'd start talking about death.

I got that she felt guilty because she thought her daughter was dead. Not to mention the fact that her nigga was gone too. We hadn't talked about what happened that night. We had been together every day for damn near a week. Tomorrow, I had business to handle, so my mans was goin' to have to come and sit with her.

Once we were in the truck, Gia wasted no time firing up a blunt that she had left in the ashtray. I watched the way she glared out the window at the people parked next to us as the woman got her daughter into her car seat. Every time we were out and a baby was near, she just stared at them. I had to cuss a few people out for sayin' something to her. Even though the shit was creepy as hell, I knew why she was doing the shit, and as long as she was out with me, nobody was goin' to say shit to her about it.

"Where are we goin'?" Gia asked as I passed the exit to go to the house where she'd been staying at.

"What happened the night you was with them niggas?" I asked, turning down the music and ignoring her question.

What she said would determine how this was going to go.

"They were supposed to be taking me to get something to eat. Every day, I wish that I would have just ordered a pizza, then maybe things wouldn't have went the way they did. We were on our way to pick up my food at Village Inn, and Joe spotted your truck. I didn't think nothin' of it. I had one headphone in my ear and wasn't really paying attention to what they were talking about until I noticed that Brad was doing lines.

"Next thing I knew, we were following y'all, and Brad was so high out of his mind that everything I said was going in one ear and out the other. Joe was driving, and his sights were set on y'all, so my food was out of the question. You're a target, and I'm sure you already know that. I didn't hear them say it, but you know that any nigga that isn't on y'all side that wants to be and knows they can't wants to take y'all out. Right?"

"Was Brad your daughter's dad?" I asked.

"Yeah."

I made my way to Nana's. It took us about twenty minutes to make it there. Gia sang along to the songs that came from the speakers. When music was playing, Gia seemed to relax a little and wasn't so tense. I knew that it took a lot for her to talk about that night.

I could tell by her facial expressions when she talked about Brad that she loved the nigga. But any nigga that would be doing lines with his baby momma in the car didn't give a fuck, and then to try to hit a lick and put her in harm's way like that, he didn't give a fuck bout her or the baby. Now wasn't the time to get into all that, but I knew eventually it was going to need to be said in order for us to be able to get anywhere.

"Look, I can't change the way that shit went down that night. To be real with you, I don't give a fuck about them niggas, neither one of 'em. You got two choices. You can just do exactly what I say and go in here and get your daughter, or I can drop you off and see about your body being found tomorrow morning on the news?" I asked as soon as I killed the engine.

"My daughter is still alive?" she asked with her voice and hands literally shaking.

"You need to understand that you're goin' to have to do exactly what I tell you to do. I know this is goin' to be hard to for you, but not doing so will have you and your daughter having a double funeral."

"Thank you so much, Gunna. I'll do whatever you want me to do," Gia pleaded, unbuckling her seat belt and wrapping her arms around my neck, huggin' me tight.

"Alright, get off me because I need to make sure that you understand. One fuck up, and I won't be able to guarantee you and your daughter's safety," I said, and Gia quickly let me go.

I could tell by the way that she moved and jumped when somebody was talkin' that she'd been abused. I could move my fuckin' arm, reachin' over her to grab something, and she was jumping. I didn't even know nothin' about the nigga Brad, but I was sure he was probably kickin' her ass. Bitches loved and clung to niggas that kicked their ass, and that was some shit that I would never understand. I knew somebody that I used to be close to that had similar characteristics years after being away from her abuser.

"Whatever I need to do, I'll do it. Can we go in so I can get my daughter?" she asked, growing impatient.

I got out, and she followed close behind. I didn't waste any more time giving her any more information. The less she knew right now, the better. How eager she was to get in the house and get Kiara, I knew that what she said about doing whatever, she meant that.

"I know you been seeing me calling you, muthafucka! And who the hell is this you are bringing in my house? Because you know them bitches that you be fuckin' with don't wash they ass right and—" Nana said before I cut her off as soon as we came in the house.

"Nana, why would you say some shit like that? What's wrong with you?" I asked.

"So, who the fuck are you?" Nana asked while staring at Gia, waiting for an answer.

"My name is Gionna," Gia replied after lookin' at me, shocked by Nana's mouth.

"Gina, you ain't got no ass at all," Nana advised her like she didn't know how big her ass was.

Gia didn't say anything, even though I knew she wanted to because she bit down on her glossed lip. Her fuckin' up her name had her feelin' a way, way more than the fact that she commented 'bout her not having much ass. She had some sexy ass lips. I shook the thoughts that were coming to my mind. Right now, I had to focus. Once I figured out how I was going to bring this shit to my brother, then I'd make my move, because I knew that Gia wasn't goin' to be as easy as the other females on my team.

"So, why the fuck did you bring her over here?" Nana asked me but was lookin' at Gia.

"I'm here to get my baby," I advised her.

"So, you think that you're going to come and take that baby out of here, and it's twenty degrees outside? I don't fuckin' think so," Nana said.

"Nana, she has a coat. I have heat in my truck. She'll be good."

"You heard what I said, and you already know how I feel about anybody that isn't Maddie, so you knew that bringing her in here wasn't a good idea."

"Kiara, is upstairs in the first room on the left. You can go pack up her stuff," I told Gia, tryin' to hurry up and get the fuck out of here.

"Utt unn, Gina, don't take another step. I don't know you. You won't be goin' past this living room. You might steal somethin'. If you weren't fuckin' this nigga, I might would have let you make me some shrimp fried rice, but any bitch would give him some pussy is nasty, nasty," Nana said.

I knew that Nana wasn't goin' to let up, and if Gia took another step, Nana was liable to pull out the twenty-two that she kept close by at all times.

"Have a seat," I said, gesturing for Gia to sit down since she was holding up the wall.

"Utt unn, homegirl. Keep standing," Nana interjected.

"Nana, why are you trippin' with her? She doesn't know you, and you never met her," I asked, getting up to go and get the baby.

"I know a hoe when I see one. She not just a regular hoe either! Don't come in my muthafuckin house standin' up for some bitch that you've known for two seconds."

"Tokyo, Jackie Chan, are you scared?" Nana asked Gia.

"Not at all," Gia said, folding her arms across her chest.

Nana hopped out of her seat fast as hell, and the sudden movements caused Gia to jump, and Nana noticed. She shook her head and made her way over to me, grabbin' me by my arm and pullin' me out the room.

"What the hell are you doing with her battered and abused ass? What the fuck do you do, go and find abused bitches and try to save 'em? You ain't fuckin' Superman, and I know yo' big ass can barely walk from room to room. What the fuck is goin' on? And don't fuckin' lie!" Nana said once we were in the kitchen.

Once Daisey came runnin' into the kitchen, I was in the clear to get the fuck on. Because she knew that I wasn't goin' to tell her anything in front of the kids. I made my way out the room as Nana started fussing with Daisey about somethin'. When I heard the back door open, I knew that Honey was here once I heard Nana start cussing.

"I'll be right back," I told Gia as I made my way back through the living room and upstairs to get Kiara.

Once I got upstairs, I threw some shit into Kiara's diaper bag and then put her in her car seat. I snatched up a teddy bear and blanket and then made my way downstairs. Nana was still in the kitchen goin' off on Honey, so I ushered Gia out the door. I hit the locks on my truck, and Gia hopped in the back seat. I got Kiara in the back seat and then got the fuck on before Nana realized that I was gone.

As much as Nana was complaining about Kiara, I knew that she was growing attached to her. She really didn't want her to leave. I was her favorite grandchild. Honey used to be, but she fucked that up a long time ago. I knew that I was goin' to have to hear Nana's mouth some more about taking Kiara, but right now, I needed to make sure that Gia understood how things were goin' to go.

My phone vibrated, and lookin' down at it as I sat at a red light, I saw it was my brother.

"So, when did you decide you were taking the police on vacation with you?" I asked because he damn sure never mentioned that.

"Get on the next flight out here, ASAP," Nightmare spat and ended the call.

"I need to tell you somethin'. I don't know how you're gon' react, but I really have to get this off my chest since I feel like you're risking a lot for me and my daughter," Gionna said as I looked at her through the rearview mirror.

"What's up?" I asked, because she just stopped talkin'.

"Your grandma was right about one thing she said... Well, things weren't all sweet between me and Brad. I used to have to make money at times doing things that I'm not proud of and—"

"What, you were selling pussy?" I asked, because my Nana said she wasn't just a regular hoe.

"I was an escort and—"

"A prostitute?"

"Look, I have a lot of enemies, and with my affiliation with Brad, I don't even know them all. I just had to let you know."

"Is there anything else that I need to know?"

As she talked, I was listening, but I stopped lookin' at her to be real. I just couldn't look at her anymore. I gave my attention to the road. Here I was settin' shit up to risk it all to keep her and her daughter alive, and I had no idea until now who the fuck she really was. I didn't know why the fuck Nightmare needed me in Mexico, but if he knew the shit that she just told me, then it was about to be a fuckin' issue. A few minutes passed, and the only thing that could be heard was the wind blowing hard and Kiara's light snores.

"Are you going to send your brother to kill us?" Gia asked, rockin' the baby in her arms, making me look at her in the rearview mirror.

I didn't respond. My phone vibrated with a text message from Honey saying that Maddison was in the hospital. I already knew why she was in the hospital and Honey knew just like Maddison that I was not goin' up there to see her. I was sure Honey was in her feelings, but I had other shit that needed my attention.

My actions hurt Maddison's parents, who didn't do anything to anybody and treated me like I was their child. They didn't deserve what happened to them, and no amount of money that I gave Maddison would bring them back. I couldn't save Ike because he crossed a line that he shouldn't have crossed. Every time I saw his baby momma or one of his kids, that shit hurt my heart.

Gia and her daughter didn't have shit to do with what Brad chose to do. I'd done a lot of fucked-up shit that had hurt a lot of people. I might do some shit tomorrow that was gon' shake somebody's whole world, but when I could do good, I did. The feelings that I caught for Gia weren't part of the plan, but I just had to play this shit smart and see how it went. I needed to see where her head was at while I tried to figure out how I was gon' handle this shit with my brother.

"Yo' sister ever fucked with a thug?" I asked.

"What, you tryin' to fuck my sister? She's not interested in being a part of yo' flock of bitches. You a disrespectful ass nigga," Gia spat.

"You ain't got on no granny panties," Maurice said as I stood in front of him, lookin' over the balcony.

I looked back at him, rolling my eyes, and turned back around looking at the ocean.

"What did you want to talk about?" I asked, because he asked me to come to his room after I was already in mine and comfortable.

He pulled me down onto his lap, and I didn't put up a fight or say anything. I just leaned back and got comfortable as I inhaled his cologne. I kept telling myself that I shouldn't be here, but I hadn't even attempted to leave. If my job found out, then I wouldn't have one. I got a text message from Ervin from a texting app, telling me that he knew that I was with the "thug". How he had been attempting to break me, I knew that he was willing to get even dirtier with our divorce. I knew that he wouldn't hesitate to ruin my job for me if he knew that Maurice was the father of a client.

"What's goin' on with you?" he asked.

"Just thinking about this stuff with finding a place. All of this is nice, and I'm not tryin' to seem ungrateful, but I don't have a home, Maurice. I'm living out of two suitcases in a hotel. That's not your problem, so let's talk about something else."

"What do you want from a man? Because I'm gon' be real with you. I'm not goin' with you to get yo' hair and nails done. I'm not holding yo' purse or no goofy shit like that."

"Shut up. I would never ask you to carry my purse. Maurice, I don't know if this is a good idea. Your daughter is a client of mine. I've never had an issue with working in the gray area because of the type of work that I do, but this is definitely crossing that."

"If that was how you felt, then why the fuck did you come here?"

I leaned up and looked back at him with my elbows in his bare chest.

"I can go," I suggested, and he quickly let me out of our embrace.

"I'm not tryin' to interfere with what you have goin' on with yo' job, and if you feel that's the case, then we don't need to go no further with this."

I didn't say anything because lately, I hadn't been liking the way things have been goin' with my job. The way they had been handling some of these kids I did not agree with. It was only so much that I could do, and I'd had to realize that I couldn't save everyone. My phone started vibrating, and I looked down at it. It was Amayah asking me could she come in my room to talk to me. I showed Maurice the message, and he nodded his head.

"What are you waiting for? Go and see what my baby wants," he said.

"We still need to talk, Maurice," I said as I got up.

"Milan, I'm not goin' nowhere, but I'm goin' to tell you now. I don't give a fuck about yo' fuckin' job," he said while lighting a cigar.

"Fuck it. I'll go and see if my baby is okay," he said, getting up like I was taking too long.

I made my way out back into the room. As I made my way to Amayah's room, she called me crying. I told her that I was on my way to her and got her off the phone. I picked up my speed and made my way across the hall to Amayah's room. Before I could knock on the door, it swung open, and Amayah fell into my arms.

Amayah was huggin' me tight, and her tears are wetting up my dress. She hadn't said anything about the boy that had been puttin' her through it in a while, but I knew that was what it was about with the way that she was crying. I got her over to the bed with no help from her. The sad music that she had blasting throughout the room wasn't making her feel any better.

Amayah scooted to the middle of the bed, and I noticed

bruises all over her arms and as I looked her over good, I noticed that she has several big bruises all over her caramel skin.

"Amayah, is he putting his hands on you?" I asked, and she started crying and buried her face into her hands.

This explained why she didn't want to go swimming and was fully covered at dinner, when it was burning hot here. She kept complaining about being cold whenever her dad said anything to her about having on extremely hot clothes. It all made sense why he had the hold on her that he had. She told me that they were done, and she hadn't talked to or seen him, but clearly that was a lie. I tried to console her, and she got sick of the sad music and screamed for Alexa to stop the music.

"Amayah, I'm sure that you don't want to hear this because you clearly care about—"

"Please, Milan, you cannot tell my dad. Please, please, you cannot tell my dad," she begged.

"This is something that you need to tell your dad. I can't get in the middle of this with y'all."

Amayah started crying and layin' her head on my shoulder. I consoled her and after about ten minutes, she calmed down and made her way to the bathroom to get herself cleaned up. As the bathroom door closed, my phone started vibrating with a text message from Maurice.

Maurice: Is my baby okay?

Me: She is going to be fine.

Maurice: Then what the hell is taking you so long.

From the day that Maurice showed up to the hotel that I was staying at, I had seen another side of him. He remembered what types of food that I enjoyed, and Ervin couldn't even tell you how I liked my eggs. He was still rude as hell, and I never knew what he was going to say, but I knew that he had nothing to gain from tryin' to pursue me. He was secure and had made a wonderful life for him and his daughter, and here I was, tryin' to pick up the pieces of mine.

"Can you stay in here with me until I fall asleep?" Amayah asked as she jumped in the bed, taking me away from my thoughts.

"Yeah, I will," I said as Amayah got comfortable in the bed turning on the TV.

After about twenty minutes, she was sleep before the movie even started good.

Knock, knock, knock.

I know it was nobody but Maurice. I slipped out of the bed and made my way to the door.

"Is my baby—"

"She's fine," I lied and grabbed his hand and attempted to pull him away.

He had his foot wedged in the door.

God, please don't let this man go into this room.

"She's asleep. I know you hear her snoring," I said, pulling his arm, but his feet were still planted on the ground.

"Why you in such of rush all of sudden? And why the fuck did you leave me on read?" he asked as he quietly closed the door.

"I thought you didn't text?" I asked as I led the way to his room.

"You don't have to fuckin' worry about it because I'll never text yo' ass again," he said and wrapped his arms around my waist as we walked into his room.

I knew he doesn't text anybody except Amayah, and he had made that clear from the first time that I met him. Now, he was texting me, and just that fast, he'd never text me again. To be as mean as he was, he was real sensitive. If shit didn't go his way when he wanted, he had no issue shutting shit down.

"Oh, my, you did all this?" I asked as I looked up and noticed the candles burning and rose petals and balloons that filled the room.

I turned around, and Maurice had the same facial expression he always had... a mean one.

"Do you ever smile?" I asked.

"As long as the people around me are good and smiling, that's all that matters," he replied.

I looked around the room at the rose petals and burning candles in amazement. I couldn't lie and say that I wasn't impressed, because I was. The fact that he had sections strategically placed around the room with all the things that I liked, which was never somethin' that I even mentioned to him; nobody has never done anything like this for me before.

One of the tables was filled with purses and wallets from all my favorite designers. The couch was filled with shoe boxes. I'd always been into shoes, but growing up, I never was able to keep up with the latest, but as soon as Ervin started getting money, I would buy every shoe my heart desired. Heels were cute, but I only wore them when I absolutely had to.

Another table was set up and filled with jewelry, everything that you can imagine. Even with the room just being lit by candlelight, it was glistening, and all of my favorites were all lined out.

"Maurice, you really didn't have to do all of this," I advised him.

"You need to learn how to let a man be a man. I know what I have to do and what I don't have to do. You need somebody around you that's adding to you. You give out so much and don't get the same back in return. Let me do that for you."

"This is coming from a man that wouldn't even pay for my meals?" I said, laughing as he wrapped his arms around my waist as I made my way around the room.

Monica's "Superman" played throughout the room. The music wasn't too loud or too low. It was just right. My thoughts drifted to the possibilities of Maurice being able to be my Superman. From what I'd seen from him, he definitely had a lot of the qualities that I would want in a man. I was oo-ing and ah-ing over one of the dresses that Maurice had gotten me, and he turned me to face him.

He snatched the dress out of my hand and threw it over the rack the clothes were hanging on. He ripped my dress off of me and threw it on the ground. Wrapping his arms around me, he hugged me tight in between kissin' me and guiding me to the bed. Whatever he wanted to do, we could do. As his hands caressed my body, I felt a feeling that I had never felt before.

He pushed me onto the bed and dropped to his knees, rippin' off my panties swiftly. He wasted no time diving head-first into my wetness that he was the reason behind. The way he flicked his tongue was like no other. I mean, I didn't have but one person to compare it to, but I'd never experienced this feeling he was giving me before. Within seconds, my body was shaking, and he didn't let that slow him up. He just kept goin' for what felt like forever, until he had decided that I'd had enough.

As he came out of his clothes, I watched and admired his body. Just like I figured, his chest was covered in tattoos, from tribal pieces and portraits to quotes. As he took off his boxers, I wasn't prepared or expecting the dick that he had. The thickness made my mouth water and my pussy pulsate. He grabbed a box of condoms out of the drawer and quickly got one and slipped it on.

Maurice roughly snatched me to the end of the bed and dove into me like he had been waiting all of his life to enter my walls. With each stroke he gave me, it sent chills up my spine.

"Mauriiice..." I cried out in pleasure as he pulled my left leg over his shoulder and went deeper, causing me gasp as tears of pleasure fell from my eyes.

The way that Maurice was handling my body was an experience that I never imagined was possible. As we continued to switch positions, I was ready to tap out. His drive and dedication to satisfy me was somethin' that he was showing me in every way. I waited with the perfect arch, preparing myself for him to enter as I felt his tongue enter my ass.

"Shit, Maurice!" I cried out, and he just kept on goin'.

"I'm gon' tell you right now, if this ain't what you want, then we can agree to be cool for Amayah's sake, and I'll back the fuck off," Maurice said as I drank some water.

"You ask me that after what you just did?" I said, smiling from ear to ear.

"If you are goin' to be with me, you have to be with me and only me. I'm not sharing shit. I have to be able to trust you and know that you can be my peace. I don't need any more hell," Maurice seriously replied.

I took in everything that Maurice said, and as I came back to reality, I knew that he was serious. I also knew that there was no way that I could tell him about Ervin. I had plenty of time to tell him, and the thought of losing him wasn't somethin' that I could stomach.

Chapter Thirteen

NIGHTMARE

"**D**ad, so you and Milan are together?" Amayah asked as she came bustin' in my room like the fuckin' police.

"Stay out of my business, Amayah. I thought y'all were goin' to the spa."

"We are. Milan is still getting dressed. Thank you so much, Dad, for lettin' me still come. I thought you were going to come without me."

"I thought about it, but you done turned shit around. I take you somewhere every Valentine's Day. Even though I should have just brought yo' ass somethin' from Walgreens."

"Dad, you didn't make Milan pay for her room, did you?"

"Why?"

"That's so embarrassing. Please tell me that you didn't do

that. I hope you got her a gift too. Because how are you goin' to give me a gift and not give her nothin'?"

"Gift, girl this is yo' gift. What would make you think that you are getting a gift?"

"You didn't get me nothin'?" Amayah asked, poutin'.

I didn't even respond. I got up and made my way out on the balcony. I got her fuckin' gift, but I shouldn't have. She damn sure shouldn't have been expecting one. I'd always gotten her a gift on Valentine's, and we'd been going to a different country since she was six. I never wanted my baby to be impressed by a nigga and their little money. When a nigga could move a bitch with money, he didn't have to put in work and do the little things that mattered. Any nigga that stepped to her should have to put in work to be able to get any of her time.

"Are you still talkin' to that nigga?" I asked as Amayah walked out onto the balcony.

"Dad, what is the lawyer saying about my case? Why can't I just take a plea? I'm tired of goin' to court. I just want this to be over," Amayah said, draping her arms over the rails.

"It's going to be over soon. I have a meeting when we get back home. Once I get you out of this shit, you need to know that this shit can't happen again. No nigga that gives a fuck about you would ever put you in this type of position. I hope you understand that," I said as she looked over at the ocean.

"I do," Amayah pouted.

"What's wrong?"

"Nothin' really, but my mom has been calling."

Amayah never really talked to me about her mom, but as I listened to her talkin' I knew that she is feelin' a way about her momma not being around. I hadn't seen or heard anything about Nadia since I cussed her ass out and made her leave the cheerleading competition. Even though I'd rather not talk to the bitch, when I got home, I was goin' to go and see her so we could get to the bottom of a few things.

I knew what the fuck I went through with not having my parents around, and I never wanted Amayah to go through any of that. Nadia wanted to go out every weekend and run the streets with her friends. Shit, I would come home some nights after trappin', and she would still be in the streets. When I started getting money, the first thing I did was moved my family out the hood. Nadia wasn't feelin' it; she was then and is now a hood rat.

I loved her ass, and it wasn't nothin' that I wouldn't have done for her, but when I was tryin' to elevate, she was tryin' to just get a purse and her nails done. It just got to the point where I wasn't happy, and I didn't want her around me. I just wanted to raise our daughter together, and everything else really didn't matter. Nadia had other plans.

"Are you goin' to call her back?" I asked after Amayah finished venting.

"I'll call her back when we get home."

"Look, I don't want you to get your hopes up just because I brought ol' girl out here. Or because you thought you seen us kissing. Because—"

"Dad, stop playin'. Y'all was definitely kissing. I know how you are, and the fact that you are helping her look for a house... You don't like nobody, and you're not goin' out your way to help nobody if it's not us. I know that you like her. I never even seen you with a girl besides my mom. You need to just move her in, and y'all can get married so you can stay out my business."

"I'm gon' always be in yo' business. I don't care what I'm doin' or where you at. When you're thirty, I'm gon' be in yo' business. I ain't goin' nowhere. I'm gon' be in yo' business forever, baby."

"So, you do want to get married? I mean, you is old, and you can't live with me and my husband and or kids. So you need somebody—"

Knock, knock, knock.

"Dad, can I get yo' card?" Amayah asked in between runnin' into the room.

"You ain't ever getting married, and you ain't having no fuckin' kids! Where the hell is yo' card?" I asked as she opened the door for Milan.

"Dad, you know you took my cards."

Milan came into to the room, and Amayah was whining about me giving her my credit card, but I wasn't payin' any attention to her. I was lookin' at Milan, and she was smiling from ear to ear. I can't lie; I didn't know if it was this fuckin' air out here or what, but she was lookin' good as hell, homeless and all.

I can't lie; she was a real one, and she'd damn near become

a part of the family. She showed me who she was when she came to me about the feds steppin' to her. I laid back to see how she handled that information, and she kept it cool. She never even brought it up again, which surprised me. I wasn't the type of nigga that jumped headfirst into some shit, so I was gon' take my time and see how shit played out.

I was tryin' to handle shit different when it came to Milan. I didn't do a background check on her or get her pussy facts. In the past, I'd done that shit, and it didn't get me no damn where. Word could come back and tell me that the bitch was perfect and wasn't nothin' wrong with her, and then she'd switch up. She was showing me that she was real, and if that shit was an act, then eventually I'd see. Because what's done in the dark will come to the light.

"Come on, Amayah," Milan said.

"Dad, give me the card." Amayah whispered as she walked up on me as I sat on the bench.

"I got it, before yo' daddy be sending me a bill for that," Milan said.

"Ugh, Dad, that is so embarrassing. You sent her a bill? Who does that?" Amayah asked and made her way out the room.

"I ain't send her no damn bill. But if she keeps talkin' shit, I'm goin' to send her ass one!" I yelled before the door closed behind them.

At first, I wasn't feelin' her, and I got really territorial when it came to my baby. I wasn't really feeling her job, but after hearing her talk to Amayah, I knew that she really gave a fuck about the kids. I also knew that she didn't want to do that police shit forever, so that was even better. But being around her every other day, she started to grow on a nigga. No matter how much shit I talked, she didn't let that deter her from coming around and being there for Amayah. Amayah talked to her more than she talked to me.

My daughter was very attached to her, and I didn't want her to get her hopes up about us and things not work out. This situation was never somethin' that I thought I would end up in. If she knew the truth about me, I didn't think she would fuck with me like that. Gunna had been handling the streets, so he handled the situation with her sister and niece. If she knew that I was behind the shit, I knew that she would never talk to me and probably would cut ties with Amayah. I knew that would break my baby's heart, so I couldn't let that happen.

I stood ten toes on all the shit that I did. If Gia would have done what I told her to do, then we wouldn't have had to take it this far, but she decided to go missing. There is a consequence for every decision, and we all had to live with that shit.

I got up and made my way over to the desk on the other side of the suite and powered on my work phone. We were supposed to go to Jamaica, but I needed to meet up with my plug to discuss business. Gunna better have his ass here on the first flight tomorrow. I pushed our meeting back because he needed to handle some shit in the streets. He'd been stepping up and even falling back from all his bitches, so I knew that he's taking this shit serious.

———

"So, when is the wedding?" Gunna asked.

"I know right. I can be the maid of honor, because she doesn't have any friends. She's mean like my dad," Amayah threw in.

"I'm not mean," Milan added.

"Alright, we gotta go," I said, because we had to meet Lady Heroin in thirty minutes.

"Nigga, damn, I'm hungry," Gunna complained.

"What the fuck is new? Missing a meal wouldn't hurt yo' big ass," I suggested as he stuffed his face.

"I'm sick of this fuckin' family. I'm 'bout to go find me a bitch so I can start a new fuckin' family," Gunna said, gettin' up from the table and then stuffing some bacon in his mouth.

Amayah and Milan were laughin'.

"I'll get with y'all when I get back," I said as Amayah jumped up to hug me with one hand and her free hand out.

"Yo' stepmom got you, baby," I said as I kissed Amayah on the forehead while lookin' at Milan.

Her face turned red, and I knew that caught her off guard. Gunna started choking on his bacon, and Amayah squeezed me tighter. I patted her on her back so she can let me the fuck go. I had shit to do. I slipped some money into Amayah's purse. When she went to put on some lip gloss, she'd see it.

"So you can just move with us," Amayah sang, runnin' over to Milan who hadn't taken her eyes off me.

"Why would you say that?" Milan mouthed, and I walked away, leaving her mind wondering.

Gunna and I made our way out of the restaurant. Lady H's driver was waiting for us in the front. I hated the way this muthafucka drove when she wasn't in the car. Just fuck us and our lives, but if she was in the car, this nigga drove like he had precious cargo.

"So, what's goin' on with y'all?" Gunna asked as we made our way through the lobby.

"None of yo' fuckin' business," I spat as Jorge, the driver, let us in the limo.

"Since when you get so sensitive about a girl that you don't give a fuck about? Since when it ain't my business? You always in my damn business. Not to mention, she not a fed, so she can't help us with business," Gunna said while lightin' a blunt.

"I don't give a fuck 'bout you and none of them broke ass bitches you fuck with. I just think that you shouldn't be making every bitch you fuck feel special. But that's yo' business as long as it doesn't start fuckin' with mine."

"What you think Kay gon' say if she finds out 'bout Milan?"

"Kay knows what the fuck it is between us. I ain't never told her that it would be no more or no less. I see Kay after the sun goes down. I'm not taking Kay on dates or shopping sprees. I ain't you, nigga," I reminded him as Jorge slammed on the brakes.

"Damn, is you tryin' to fuckin' kill us!" I spat.

"Shut the fuck up. That nigga got a fuckin' Draco on the seat up there. I ain't dying in Mexico because you don't know how to talk to people," Gunna threw in.

"You should've stayed yo' ass on the porch if you don't like how I talk," I replied as I sat back to prepare for this meeting.

After about ten minutes, we made it to Lady H's estate. I'd been here a few times since she moved here, but I couldn't lie it was nice. It made my shit look small. Gunna rolled down the window, lookin' in amazement as we rode up the long driveway to her home.

"Damn, she got shooters all around this bitch," Gunna said as one of the men she had watching her home nodded his head at us.

Once we made it to main house, I didn't wait for Jorge to open the door for us; I got out. Gunna's big ass shut the door.

"This nigga," I said, shaking my head as Lady H came outside.

"I'm supposed to be retired, and I can't retire because you don't know how to work with other people," Lady H said as she walked over to me.

Jorge took his time getting out to let Gunna out. That nigga wasn't goin' to budge until he opened the door. I didn't know who the hell Gunna thought he was. Jorge finally opened the door as Lady H and I had small talk.

"We were supposed to be married. You know you broke my heart, right? Just fuck me, huh? After all that we done been through. I would never do you like that!" Gunna said as he got out the car and walked over to us.

"You betta stick to playin' with them lil' girls because I'd have to kill yo' ass," Lady H replied and led the way into her house.

"I would never play with you. We could have had a baby if that's what you wanted. That's all you had to say, and we could have made that happen, Baby H!"

I hoped her fuckin' husband wasn't here, because this nigga just didn't know when to shut the fuck up. Every time he saw her, they played this game, and she played right along with him. He didn't care who it was, if it was a woman around, he has to say somethin' to her. Luckily, she liked him; otherwise, he would have been swimming with the fishes years ago.

We made it to the second floor and into the conference room where Lady H did business, with her and Gunna goin' back and forth about a love affair that never fuckin' happened. Lady H was known for not playin' games and being all about business with everybody, even her own kids, but when it came to Gunna, she'd play all damn day.

"So, are you ready?" Lady H asked Gunna, gettin' to business after a few minutes.

"I'm always ready. So when the fuck are you getting a divorce?"

"Never, you fuckin' psycho. You need to focus and be serious," Lady H suggested.

We were sitting around a big round table. I looked around

the room at the pictures that she had of her and her family all around the room. From what she had told me over the years about her family, I was surprised that she fucked with any of them that she had left. The pictures hangin' up were mostly of her grandkids and her daughter. When she found out she was pregnant, she claimed that she was retiring, but that wasn't goin' to work for me. She put her stepson in charge, but I didn't do new niggas.

"What the fuck am I supposed to be ready for?" Gunna asked, lookin' at me.

"To run shit on yo' own. Nightmare is preparing for retirement. If he's out, you're goin' to have to be ready to step up."

"When the fuck did you decide this?" Gunna questioned, with his attitude evident.

"I'm gon' let y'all talk. I'll be back," Lady H said and made her way out the room.

"So, when the fuck was you gon' tell me that you were leaving the game?" Gunna asked once the door closed behind Lady H.

"This shit ain't forever, nigga. You already know that. Amayah asked when I was gon' be done. I told her to give me some time. What difference do it fuckin' make? Nigga, you actin' like I'm not gon' see yo' ass every day or if you need me, I'm not gon' pull up!"

"So, are you tryin' to leave for Amayah or that bitch? Because all of a sudden, you are inviting her on trips, and then you are planning for retirement."

"Milan doesn't have shit to do with this. Don't call her out her muthafuckin name. I don't know why the fuck you in yo' feelings. I've talked about leaving this shit before. What the fuck I'm supposed to do, wait until I'm old and gray nigga?"

"Do whatever the fuck you gon' do," Gunna said, leaning back in his chair.

After about five minutes, Lady H came back in the room. We discussed the changes with the shipments. She could feel the tension in the room, and Gunna got a call that he had to take, so he made his way out of the room.

"So, who is she?" Lady H asked.

"Amayah."

"Nigga, how long have I known you? I know that it's not your daughter. You've been doin' this shit, and it's never come in between you being an active father. You might can try that shit with somebody else, but I know you. It's some woman, and she must be the truth, because it takes a lot to move you. You been lookin' at my big, beautiful ass for years and haven't even tried.

"Nigga, I know I'm the truth and the light, so what the fuck is she doing to you? I understand that you get tired. This shit will drain you, and no matter what you give to this shit, it will never give it back to you, but yo' brother isn't ready. I'm not tryin' to tell you what to do. The choice is yours, but that nigga doesn't even have a solid foundation at home. How the fuck is he goin' to handle this shit?

"I know that you have him handling shit now. How is that going? Because how the fuck can you handle business and six bitches?"

I listened to everything Lady H was sayin', and maybe she was right. I wanted Gunna to not even be involved in this shit. I kept him out of it as long as I could. I wanted Gunna to go to college and play football. He was offered a full ride scholarship, but he didn't want to go. After talking to him for months, finally he agreed to go and visit the college.

We went to visit the college, and when we came back, I ended up getting locked up. I damn near begged Gunna to go, so he finally gave in and went. I ended up gettin' out of jail after about two months, and Gunna was back at home. Come to find out, he got accused of some shit that he didn't do and just left. I talked to his ass every day, and he kept lying saying everything was good and he was in school.

So once I got home, I kicked his ass out. Honey cried for days, and Nadia begged me to let him come home. After a month of him sleeping on Ike's couch, I let him come home. Under one condition—he had to get a job, and that shit lasted not even a month. Before I knew it, he was at the house on the couch more than me. He begged me to just work for me, so I gave him a chance, and next thing I knew, he was knee deep in and never had any plans of getting out.

"Let me guess. Milan doesn't know who Nightmare is, does she?" Lady H asked.

"Naw, she doesn't," I admitted.

"Well she did go to college, and didn't the feds step to her? She can't be that damn dumb. I mean, the feds ain't asking questions about no real estate tycoons that I know. She knows that you're into something other than that; she has to. What's goin' on with that? What's Iman saying?"

"Shit, nothin'. They are always goin' to ask about me. That's just the way this shit goes. I haven't gotten a call about an indictment, so shit, I ain't worried. It's business as usual."

"They're coming," Lady H said, tappin' her fingers.

I nodded my head, and Gunna made his way back into the room.

"Y'all need to talk and figure this shit out. Y'all family, and even though most of mine ain't shit, I do know that Nightmare has busted his ass and gave up shit that he wanted to solidify his position in this shit. Whether you want to admit it or not, he's the only reason you're in the same room with me.

"It looks like y'all will be in this shit together for now. So, if y'all can't figure this shit out, everything is goin' to crumble. If the head of the body ain't right, then the rest is a vegetable. If y'all not on the same page, how the fuck do y'all think the rest of the team is goin' to be moving? Figure this shit out, because I'm only still even involved in this shit on the strength of Nightmare.

"I'm good, and when I'm dead and gone, everybody that shares my last name will be good. So figure it out before you have to find a new table to sit at," Lady H said, getting up and making her way out the room.

"So, what's it gon' be?" Gunna asked once Lady H was out the room.

"When I get back home, it's time to have a sit down with

everybody. Anybody that can't roll with what's about to happen is goin' to have to be laid down. We can't take no chances of nothin' happening that isn't sanctioned.

"Nigga, I'm goin' to tell you this now. I don't give a fuck if they have been yo' best friend all of your life, or you fuckin' they bitch, baby momma, or wife. Anybody that could be a fuckin' issue are gone and no coming back."

I could see Gunna's mind runnin', but he hadn't said anything. I knew that he wasn't ready now, and to be real with myself, I didn't know if he ever would be. But at the end of the day, if I had to stay in this shit, I had to make choices to guarantee that no matter what happened, we'd always be good. Bringing Milan in was a risk, but with my baby already knowing a piece, I couldn't risk hurting her more. I shouldn't have let Amayah know that anything was goin' on with us, but what was done was done.

I couldn't lie; she'd had my attention for a while. I knew that she had a good heart, and she stood ten toes on her own. I didn't have to worry about her being in the streets and on bullshit embarrassing me. But I don't know if she knew the truth if she would still be willing to even be around me, let alone sit back and ride.

"Did you handle that shit with the bitch and the baby?" I asked because he still hadn't said anything.

"Yeah, it's taken care of," he replied after a few seconds.

"Maybe if you get some fucking furniture, you can get a woman and have yo' own damn baby," I said as I stood up.

I knew that Gunna was getting attached to the baby. He

was buyin' all these toys and shit. I looked up and she had matching outfits to match the nigga, like she came out of his sac. Shit, Nana called me this morning telling me to bring the baby that she didn't even want at her house in the beginning. I didn't agree with that shit, because I knew that Nana shouldn't have been placed with the burden of taking care of the baby.

Chapter Fourteen

MILAN

I walked around the home that April insisted that I see. It was beautiful, but the price tag was something that I knew would be way more than what I was tryin' to pay. I was planning on using some of the money from the sale of my old home as a down payment and putting the rest in the bank so that I could have something to fall back on. April was really trying to convince me that this was the house for me. Everything that she was pointing out was all of the things that I loved about it already.

"I'll give you some time to look around," April said and then walked out of the living room.

The home was beautiful, and all of the furniture that was in here fit perfectly. The modern look and the color schemes in every room fit just right. The home was brand-new, and all of the things that Maurice warned me about with the other house weren't an issue here. I knew to be able to get an affordable mortgage payment, I was going to have to use all the money that was supposed to be my cushion until the divorce was settled.

Since we came back from Mexico, Maurice had been everything that I needed him to be. I was already used to being around his family, so that hadn't been an issue. I hadn't seen Christopher since we were in Mexico, which was making me think that he had an issue with me being around. They were always so close, and I very rarely saw one without the other. Now all of a sudden, it had been two weeks, and I hadn't seen him, and Maurice hadn't even mentioned him.

Maurice insisted that I stayed in one of his places until I found a home. When I declined, I came to my room, and all my stuff was gone, and the keys and a note from him were on the bed, telling me to take my ass to the house. With his job he was always busy, but he made time, and that was somethin' that I never knew I was missing until I got it. I'd never called him and he didn't answer. When I tried to handle things on my own, he was always by my side and speaking up for me at times when I didn't have the courage to do so.

I think what had pulled me into him and accepted all of him was the fact that he had started to respect my career choice. He didn't downplay what I did and belittle it compared to him and all that he had. Ervin never supported what I did, and he didn't have an issue with letting me know it every chance he got. This divorce was getting ugly and was takin' strength in me that I never knew existed. Maurice has no idea that him and his support had been the only thing that had kept me going, because I knew that if I fell, he'd be there to catch me, even if I said I didn't need him to.

I hadn't been honest with him about my situation, because I knew that it was messy. From being around him, I knew that drama wasn't something that he tolerated. If he knew what I was goin' through, he wouldn't be understanding, and I was sure that we'd be over. I couldn't take another loss right now; I'd already lost too much. I'd been thinking about just taking the offer that Ervin's lawyer sent to me so I could just be done. Me and Maurice were never supposed to be; it just happened and so fast that I didn't handle things the way I should have.

"So, what do you think about the house?" a familiar voice asked from behind me.

"You know that I love this house. I just showed it to you the other day," I said as I turned to face Maurice.

"I know, but coming in here is different than just staring at the pictures online every night, over and over," Maurice insisted.

"I also told you that this house was way over my budget. Since you remember everything, I know that you remembered that."

Maurice wrapped his arms around me, and we made our way through the house from room to room. He was not easily impressed; hell, I couldn't remember ever seeing him impressed by anything except Amayah. Well and the changes that Honey had made getting back on track with her plans.

Honey had been telling me about this project she was working on, and even thought Maurice was talkin' shit, I knew that he was proud of her.

"The seller really has some nice stuff; this is same stuff that I was showing you on Pinterest in this room," I said as we walked in the master bedroom.

"You gon' be sleepin' in here by yo'self. That small ass bed," Maurice said as I broke our embrace to sit on the bed.

It was so crazy that everything I wanted for my bedroom down to the bed is in this room.

"Did you look in the closet?" Maurice asked.

"Yeah, I did."

"Go look again," he insisted, pullin' me by my hands off the bed.

"I told you I already looked in here," I said as we walked through the closet.

"You looked over here?" Maurice said as he pulled down the plastic the owners had over a picture.

"Why would you do that? They clearly had that up there for a reason," I said, pickin' up the plastic off the floor.

As I tried to put it back up, I realized that the picture hanging on the wall was a picture that I kept in my planner of me, my dad, and Gionna.

"Why is this in here?" I asked.

"You didn't realize that everything in here is just like the pictures that you've been showing me or the same shit? Honey been working like a slave, and why else do you think I been having them demon seeds at my house? You know I can't stand them. But I know this is what you wanted.

"Before you say that you can't take it and I'm doin' too much, you don't have a choice. All yo' stuff from the apartment is already here. All yo' granny panties is in the top drawers. The locks to the place you were staying at was changed. You not about to keep stressin' or stressin' me the fuck about this house shit, so it's done. It's yours; the papers were already signed, and the check was already cashed. Check yo' email. Iman sent you over the papers so the house can be transferred to your name."

I plopped down on the chaise and cried my eyes out. It was not a day that went by that I don't think about my sister. We weren't in the best place, and I just wished that I would have handled things differently the last time I saw her at the hospital. The fact that they hadn't been able to find her or my niece had been eating at me. I tried to push it to the back of my mind, but I couldn't. I stopped answering the detectives' phone calls, because every time they called, it was the same thing; they were working on it.

"What are you crying for? I thought you would talk some shit and then give me some," Maurice said, scooping me up and sitting on the chaise with me in his lap.

I clung onto his neck as I cried for the first time in a while. I knew that his heart was in the right place, and I didn't want to seem ungrateful, but this was a lot. This was coming from a man that used to make me pay for my meals at places that he invited me to come to. Now he was buying me a house and furnished it too.

"Well, if it will make you stop fuckin' cryin', you can make a monthly payment to me until you pay it off," Maurice suggested.

"It would," I managed to say in between cryin'.

"Alright, I want cash only. I don't take checks. The city might go broke and not be able to pay you. Aren't they doing budget cuts?"

"I'm not telling you nothin' else," I said while rollin' my eyes.

"Thank you, baby. This is really a lot. You didn't have to do this. I really appreciate everything that you've done. I know that I've given you a lot of push back on... well, everything, but I know that you really do care and go above and beyond—"

I was cut off by Maurice kissing me after he wiped my last tears away.

"Well, can you cook now? You keep saying that you can cook, but I ain't seen you boil no water since I met yo' ass," Maurice said after he broke our kiss.

"Yeah, I guess I can put somethin' together. What kind of ramen noodles you want?"

"I'm not eating like I'm in jail. You must be losin' yo' mind. Probably lightheaded because you ain't ate nothin'. I have to go and talk to the lawyer about Amayah's case, and then I'll be back."

"Can I talk to you for a minute, Milan?" my supervisor Mike asked, peeking his head into my office.

"Sure, what's up, Mike?" I asked as I sent an email, updating the courts on one of my clients.

"I wanted to talk to you because we received a visit earlier when you were out doing school visits."

"A visit from who?"

"Federal Agents Clark and Burns. They wanted to talk to you, but while they were here, they brought some things to my attention that is concerning. I know how much you care about your clients. I tell you all the time that your efforts aren't goin' unnoticed. I know that you work a lot of hours that you aren't paid for.

"You go above and beyond for all your clients. Clients that don't deserve it. I've seen you treat them all the same. I know that a lot of your drive and dedication comes from your upbringing from conversations that we've had."

As Mike, went on and on about how much of a great employee that he was, I wished that he would get to the point. I didn't know why these agents wanted to talk to me again, but I still don't have anything to say. I tuned Mike out as my personal phone vibrated with a text from Amayah.

"You need to make sure that you keep your relationships with your clients and their families business only, because failure to do so puts you at risk of losing your job. You also need to take into consideration that you don't really know these people. You only know what they tell you," Mike said, still beating around the bush after a few minutes.

"Okay, and I understand," I replied.

Mike and I went over a few of my cases and discussed some issues that I was having with clients for about ten minutes. Once we finished discussing the clients, he made his way out of my office. I texted Amayah back, letting her know that I would come by the house when we left dinner. I was meeting Maurice, and checking the time, I was running late, so I gathered up my stuff and made my way out. I'm always here way later than I planned to be. When I left the house it was dark, and when I made it home, it would be dark.

When I decided to take this step to be with Maurice, I knew the risk that I was taking. Losing my job was the last thing that I needed right now, but I had grown to care about Maurice. Everything had been moving really fast, and Mike basically threatening to fire me had me questioning if I was making the right decision. I already knew what Maurice was going to say—fuck this job and do my own thing, but it was not that easy. If I left this job because of accusations of me having inappropriate relationships with clients, that was goin' to tarnish my name, so the contacts and resources that I had wouldn't do me any good because nobody would want to work with me.

I made my way out to the lobby, and I instantly got a bad feeling. I pressed the button for the elevator, and the door popped open. Two men were in the elevator, dressed down. I spoke, and the doors quickly closed. Pulling out my phone, I read an email from my attorney, saying that Ervin had denied my offer with what I was requesting. I was not surprised, and I really didn't care at this point. I didn't even respond to my lawyer; I slipped my phone into my purse and waited for the elevator to make it to the first floor.

"Nigga, fuck them niggas. Both of 'em, Nightmare and Gunna. Nigga, at this point, anybody can get it. Them and anybody that they care about. They bitches, they fuckin' seeds, they fuckin' granny, nigga, whoever! Them niggas ain't Teflon. They bleed just like us," the guy behind me to my left spat.

The elevator finally made it to the first floor, and as soon as the doors swung open, I saw Agents Clark and Burns.

"Mrs. Simmons, we see that you're in knee deep with these people, and you really have no idea who you're dealing with. The reality is, Mrs. Simmons, legally, you are still married. I have a question. Does your boyfriend know that you're married? By the look on your face I know that he doesn't know the truth about you, and I don't blame you, because you don't know the truth about him either," Clark said as him and his partner followed me through the lobby.

"You may want to hear us out, because really soon your fairytale with your knight in shining armor is goin' to come crashing down around you," Burns threw in once we were outside.

"What? What do y'all want?" I screamed out in frustration, not caring who heard or saw me.

"Can you come with us, and we can tell you everything that you need to know," Clark pleaded.

"Am I being placed under arrest?" I asked while going through my contacts to find my attorney's number.

"No, we aren't interested in arresting you. We just feel that it would be best, if we have this discussion in private," Burns whispered.

"I don't have time for this," I said and made my way to my car.

I was parked at a meter, so I was not far away from the building. Cutting through a hotel's parking lot, walking as fast as I could with Burns and Clark on my heels, my mind is racing a mile a minute. Their pleas to try to get me to come with them were falling on deaf ears. I wasn't goin' with them anywhere unless I was under arrest. They kept harassing me but had yet to even attempt to talk to Maurice.

"This is our last and final attempt, Mrs. Simmons. I'm goin' to give you until tomorrow morning to contact us to meet up. If we don't hear from you—"

Burns was cut off by me rolling up my window, but he slipped his business card in before it went all the way up. I sped off into traffic as my phone started ringing. I didn't even waste my time diggin' through my purse to get my phone. I just let it ring while thinking about what Mike said. I made my way to the restaurant to meet Maurice, even though something was telling me that I shouldn't go.

This car behind me was pissing me off, all on my ass and the car in front of me was goin' slow as hell. I looked over to my left to see if I can get over, and of course, nobody was trying to let me over. My phone started ringing again, but it was connected to the Bluetooth in my car, so I saw that it was Maurice calling. I quickly answered the call using the buttons on my steering wheel.

"Where the hell you at? Still tryin' to save the world, Superwoman?" he asked, and for some reason, just hearing his voice calmed me down.

"No, I'm on my way. I got held up at work," I replied after sighing and tryin' to relax.

"Alright, well focus on the road because you can't fuckin' drive. I'll be here," Maurice requested.

We said our goodbyes and ended the call. After about twenty minutes of strugglin' to get through traffic, which was damn near impossible, I made around the corner. I didn't know why I asked to go here, knowing that traffic would be bad this time of day.

Ding.

My gas light popped on, so I got over so I could stop at the gas station and texted Maurice, letting him know that I was around the corner. I jumped out my car and put my card in the pump to pay for my gas. Maurice tried to take my car yesterday to fill it up when he took his and Amayah's, but I hid my keys. He already did so much, and the least I could do was pay for my own gas.

"Get that bitch. What the fuck is you waiting for?" A man scoffed, and I lifted the lever so my gas could pump on its own and damn near fell tryin' to get in my car.

I didn't need to witness any damn crimes. I tried to get in my car but was stopped by someone grabbing me from behind and covering my mouth with their hand. My screams couldn't be heard, and the grip that he had on me was so tight that I couldn't move. He was strugglin' to pick me up.

"You a dumb muthafucka!" Another voice scoffed and scooped me up.

"Bitch, don't move, and I don't want to hear a mutha-fuckin peep," a familiar voice spat in my ear. We took a few steps, and he roughly threw me in a trunk and slammed it shut.

Chapter Fifteen

NIGHTMARE

How fuckin' long did it take to make it around the corner? She was always late, so this was nothin' new. I pulled out my phone and checked her and Amayah's location. Amayah is headed to the house. She was down the street from the house. It was still showing that Milan was around the corner. I threw some money on the table to pay for the drink and appetizer I ordered when she told me she was around the corner.

I jumped up to see what the fuck is going on at the fuckin' gas station. She probably ran into a fuckin' kid and was tryin' to save 'em. She thought that she could save every damn kid that she came in contact with, and when she couldn't, she would be up all night thinkin' 'bout the shit. Milan or Amayah didn't know that I had tracking devices on their car. I put one on Amayah's before she got her car back and one on Milan's car one day when she was at the house with Amayah.

It took me a few minutes to make it around the corner.

"What the fuck is goin' on?" I spat as I pulled into the gas station that was swarmed with police.

I put my tool into the secret compartment and parked my car in the first empty parking spot. I spotted Milan's car at a pump, and the pump was still in it, but I didn't see her. I walked closer and was stopped by an officer.

"Hey, where are you goin'? This is an active crime scene!" an officer yelled out.

"That's my woman's car. What the fuck is goin' on?" I spat.

"What's your name?" The officer asked.

"Maurice Rogers," I spat.

He told me to hang tight. I backed up and made my way back to my car. Reaching into my pocket, I pulled out my work phone. I called Gunna, and he answered before the phone could ring good.

"Get everybody to my house. They need to be there within an hour," I spat and ended the call, slipping the phone back in my pocket.

I waited a few minutes, and none of these fuckin' cops had come over to tell me shit. I pulled out my other phone and tried to call Milan and it was just ringing.

"Police haven't released a name as of yet, but it's clear that the abduction took place at the Shell Gas Station off of I-70. A woman was pumping gas, and that's when it happened. We will keep you updated with any new informa—" a reporter across the parking lot said, catching my attention.

They clearly weren't gon' tell me shit, so I jumped in the car and made my way to the house. With the life I lived, those that were close to me would always be a target. That was why I didn't rush to move Milan in and just got her the house that she wanted. That was also why I had been tracking her and Amayah, because I couldn't always be with them. Whoever the fuck was behind this made the biggest mistake of their lives. Wasn't no comin' back from this shit.

I pulled out my phone to make a few calls as I made my way to the house. I needed all hands on this shit. Lil' Murda ensured me that he was on the next flight out of Kansas and asked no questions when I told him that I needed him here. I made another call and didn't get an answer.

It took me about forty-five minutes to make it home, and the whole time, I was thinking about who the fuck would violate in this way. A few of the people that I requested were already here. Anybody that wasn't here within the next fifteen minutes didn't even need to come. It was not goin' to be an issue to get the people that worked for me to fall in line, but my Nana was goin' to be one.

I made my way into the house, and Amayah met me at the door.

"Where is Milan?" Amayah asked.

"I don't know," I replied, making my way in the house.

"What you mean you don't know? She said that she was

coming here after y'all went to dinner," Amayah whined, following behind me.

"Where is Faith at?" I asked, making my way to the kitchen.

"She's cooking, but, Dad, I need to talk to Milan!"

Once we made it to the kitchen, I told Amayah to sit down, and she hesitated, but she did as she was told. Faith turned around fast. The seriousness in my voice caught her attention, and I hadn't said anything to her. We hadn't ever been through no shit like this, but Faith had been around for so much shit that she knew when something was wrong.

"Somebody snatched up Milan. I need y'all—" I attempted to say but was cut off by Amayah.

"What do you mean?" Amayah questioned with tears forming in her eyes.

"I'm goin' to handle it. I haven't ever told you I was goin' to do somethin' and didn't do it. Everything is goin' to be okay, but I need you to know that some shit is about to switch up. This is to guarantee that nothin' happens to nobody else. So whatever I say, Amayah, you need to make sure that you listen and follow my instructions," I said, making my way over to Amayah and holding her as she cried into my chest.

"What do you need me to do?" Faith asked, without an ounce of worry in her voice.

"I'm goin' to have somebody to take you to get Nana, Honey, and the twins."

"Now, you know Nana is not goin' to leave her house. You

need to go and get her. She doesn't care about what's goin' on. She's not leaving her house unless you make her, and you know that," Faith replied.

"She doesn't have a choice, and I need you to get her here. I got other shit that I need to tend to. Tell her whatever the fuck you need to tell her to get her over here."

"I'll try."

"Don't try; get it done. Get yo' kids and bring 'em here too."

I helped Amayah up and escorted her out of the kitchen. I took her down the hall into my office.

"What day were you supposed to be born?" I asked once the door closed behind us.

"Huh?" Amayah questioned in between wiping her eyes.

I got her into the chair and made my way around my desk and sat down in my chair. I handed her a box of tissue and gave her a few seconds to get herself together. I knew that this is a lot for Amayah to process, but what I was getting ready to tell her was goin' to be even harder for her to process. I needed her to be able to take in everything that I said, and she could cry now, but eventually she was goin' to have to wipe away them tears.

"Amayah, the code to get into this safe is that date. You need to remember that. I've always been honest with you. Any questions that you've asked about the life that I live. A lot of things are about to happen, and it's goin' to happen fast.

"Everything is set up, so you won't have to do much. What

I need you to do is to remember everything that I have ever told you. This gun—"

"Dad, what's going on?" Amayah questioned.

"I got a call from Iman this morning. They'll be coming to get me soon, and I need you to stay on yo' shit. I'm gon' handle everything else."

"What do you mean they are coming to get you?" Amayah asked, sittin' up straight and wiping her eyes.

"What do you do under pressure?" I said, opening the safe and taking the nine and bullets out.

"Stand tall and never fold."

"What do you do if the police try to question you?" I asked, nodding my head giving her the go.

"Tell them to call you, and if they can't, call Uncle Gunna or Iman," Amayah said, checking the gun making sure the safety was on and loading it.

When Amayah turned sixteen, she had a big party and a driver's license, but before any of that took place, I sat her down and told her everything that she needed to know. She was old enough to understand, and I knew that she needed to know the truth. There had never been a day that I hadn't seen Amayah, and I moved in a way to ensure that never happened. They were coming to get me, but within a few hours I would be out.

"What if they can't call me or Gunna?" I asked.

"Tell 'em to call Fay Fay. Dad, what is goin' on? Why is this happening?"

"I don't know yet, but I need you to not lose focus. All

you need to do is what you've been doing. Don't use this shit as an excuse to start fuckin' up again. You're almost from up under this shit, and right now, I don't need to have to worry about you being back on bullshit."

Amayah and I went over everything that we needed to. All the shit that I had instilled in her, she recited word for word, not missing a beat. I prepared her for the day this might happen. She was too young to even remember the last time I was arrested.

"Come on," I said, leading the way out of my office.

"Dad, why is everybody here? I'm getting scared," Amayah said as we walked past Skitzo and Madman.

"What do people that are scared do?" I asked as me and Amayah made our way to the backyard.

I turned around and looked at her, and she was looking at the ground but hadn't answered my question.

"Amayah J'ene," I said, and she quickly lifted her head.

I held open the door for her to walk out before me.

"They make mistakes," Amayah recited.

"I know that this is a lot for you, but I need you to be a lot of shit right now, but scared isn't one of them."

We made our way out to the part of the estate that was set up as a shooting range. I looked over at Amayah and nodded my head, and she hit each target one by one. On her birthday, she had to hit each target perfectly before she could do the shit that she wanted to do. She whined and was ready to cry, but she got the shit done after a few tries.

"If a muthafucka is close, where do you aim?"

"The head, and if they are far, the legs to make 'em drop then get up on them and hit them in the head," Amayah replied.

"Damn, you hit all them, niece?" Gunna asked from behind us.

"Yeah," Amayah replied proudly.

"Let me talk to yo' dad real quick," Gunna requested, and Amayah turned to leave.

"Naw, stay right here. I need to show you one more thing," I advised her.

"Everybody is here. I need to know what the fuck you want me to do with business," Gunna asked, whispering.

I looked back at Amayah, and she was alert and listening. Gunna and I agreed that we would discuss everything together and move as one. Lady H's words were still ringing in my ears. I knew that she'd be in touch soon. I sent word to her about the indictment as soon as I got it. Lookin' back at Amayah, I nodded my head giving her the floor.

"Do you want to eat?" Amayah asked.

"Yeah," Gunna said in between laughing.

"Then you gotta get the bacon," Amayah replied with a straight face.

"Get everybody upstairs and the fuck out my living room," I said, and Gunna left me and Amayah outside.

"Dad, you gotta find Milan," Amayah said once Gunna was in the house.

I nodded my head, and we made our way back in the

house after we went over a few more things, going from room to room making sure she knew every hiding spot and she got them all on the first try. When I first went over all of this with Amayah, I didn't think that she would remember everything when she needed to, but she hadn't let me down yet.

"Go upstairs and do yo' homework," I said, and Amayah rolled her eyes, handing me the tool and hugging me tight.

I made my way to my office as my work phone vibrated in my pocket. I pulled it out and answered the blocked call.

"So what the fuck do you want?" I asked because I knew that it was the call that I was waiting for.

"We need five million. You got two hours. I'll call back within the hour with the address," the caller advised me and ended the call.

I made my way upstairs so I could get this shit over with and these niggas in the streets. When we came back from Mexico, we were supposed to be sitting down with everybody, but I hadn't planned to do it for a few days. My phone vibrated, and I got a message from Lil' Murda, tellin' me that he was about to get on a plane.

I waved Skitzo out the room, and he quickly jogged out into the hallway.

"I need you to take Faith and go to get Nana, Honey, and the twins. Bring 'em here. I don't give a fuck what you gotta do. Get them here." I instructed.

"Nigga, auntie is not gon' want to leave her house. Why not just sit one of these niggas outside her house? You know she crazy, and the last time you asked me to bring her over here for dinner, she pulled her gun out on me."

"Figure it out. This ain't fuckin' Christmas dinner. She doesn't have a choice. I need y'all niggas in the streets."

Skitzo made his way downstairs, and I knew that Nana was goin' to go off, and I was gon' have to hear about the shit for the rest of the year, but right now, I needed to know that she was okay. I couldn't take the risk of somebody being able to get to her. Hopefully, this shit would be over in a few days, and then she could go back home.

Maniac made his way in the hall without me even signaling for him to. He knew what time it was.

"What you need done?" Maniac asked.

"Go get that nigga Roc momma," I instructed.

I made my way into the conference room, and it was so quiet you could hear a penny drop in the room.

"I hope y'all slept good last night, because y'all won't be sleeping any time soon," I said as I sat down.

"How do you know that it's Roc?" Gunna asked as we sat in the parking lot of the warehouse waiting for these niggas to bring Milan.

"You fucked that nigga's wife. You don't have a bitch for him to take," I said as a black Tahoe pulled in and parked a few feet away from where my truck was.

I looked over at Gunna, and he was zoned out, staring into fuckin' space.

"Nigga, is you good? I don't got time for none of yo' bullshit right now."

"I'm good," Gunna insisted.

Whether he was or wasn't, I didn't got time to worry about that right now. He thought with his dick, and until that changed, he'd never be ready to run shit. I was losing my patience. I didn't know what the fuck was taking these two bitches so long to get out the truck. The bitch in the driver seat was a white girl, nothin' special. Blonde hair, blue eyes, and stringy, greasy hair.

The hoe in the passenger, was a well-known hood rat, Myiesha. Light skin, green eyes, and a pussy that damn near everybody done had. So now I was starting to question if it was Roc behind this shit. Considering the fact that Myiesha used to be Gunna's bitch and the terms they ended on, I didn't even have to ask why his big ass was shaking damn near making my truck rock as he watched her get out.

Gunna was jumping out before I could grab my door handle. I made my way over to the truck the bitches had gotten out of as they stood in the middle with Gunna, even though I discussed this plan with whoever the fuck was behind this shit. My stomach had been fucked up, and I got a bad feelin'. I just had to get Milan out of this trunk, right now. The windows on the truck were so dark that I couldn't see shit, and I was tryin' to.

"What the fuck is you dumb bitches doin'? Pop the fuckin' trunk!" I yelled, grippin' my tool as the trunk slowly popped open. Once the trunk was all the way open, I was met by three niggas with semi-automatic weapons pointed at me.

TO BE CONTINUED...